The Snowman Killer

Alaska Cozy Mystery
Book 1

Wendy Meadows

Majestic Owl Publishing LLC
P.O. Box 997
Newport, NH 03773

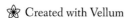 Created with Vellum

Chapter One

S arah Garland stared at the peppermint candy cane
sticking out of the mouth of a grotesque snowman.
Shielding her eyes against the icy wind, she cautiously
pushed her way through ankle deep snow, which was filled
with dark shadows emanating from the tall trees looming
overhead like white and green icicles frozen in time. The
snowman stood waiting, designed with an ugly sneer and
devious eyes carved from burnt wood, dressed in a black
leather jacket with stick arms protruding through the sleeves.
Stopping two feet away from the snowman, Sarah focused on
the peppermint candy cane as fear gripped her heart. "No," she
snapped at herself as anger replaced her fear, "I won't believe
this... I refuse to believe..."

Turning her back to the snowman, Sarah focused on her
warm, small wooden cabin. Inside the cabin, a cozy fire was
singing in a stone fireplace, sending smoke up through the
chimney toward a snowy sky. The cabin sat four miles from
town on two acres of private land, surrounded by beautiful,

natural forest that was currently covered with the whispers of winter. The cabin was Sarah's escape from the world—a private island that no man or woman could trespass on. But someone had trespassed on her island today, leaving a hideous snowman as a message to her. "Most likely it was just children," Sarah whispered aloud, in an effort to calm herself. She pulled the long, white coat she was wearing tighter against her body as the wind grabbed at her blond ponytail.

She looked toward the green Subaru parked in her driveway and wondered how long it would take her to run to it and escape to town if an intruder suddenly appeared. "Stop scaring yourself," she scolded. Turning back toward the snowman, Sarah studied the ground and began searching for boot prints. The snow was smooth. "Someone built this snowman in the dark, hours ago."

The thought of a strange figure standing in her front yard in a snowstorm building a hideous snowman as she slept, unaware, inside her cabin, made Sarah's heart begin to race. "Stop it," she scolded herself again—only this time, her voice held no true conviction. Sarah backed away from the snowman and made her way back toward the cabin. As she did, a snowball flew past her head and crashed against the passenger's side of the Subaru.

"Hey lady, nice day for a snowball fight, isn't it?" a creepy voice laughed and then vanished into the wind.

Frozen in fear, Sarah stared into the snow-covered forest running her eyes from tree to tree, searching for the voice. "Oh dear," she said and ran to her cabin. Throwing open the front door, she dashed inside, slammed the door shut, and locked it.

"Oh dear...my novel...someone is playing the part of the 'Snowman Killer'... and I'm his target."

Outside, a man wearing a black leather jacket grinned at the cabin and slithered away into the snow, tossing a frozen snowball up and down in his right hand. "Oh, the weather outside is frightful, but the fire is so delightful...and since we've no place to go...let it snow," the man began to sing.

Sarah lifted her fingers up and away from the white keyboard sitting on her old wooden writing desk that her parents had bought her when she was sixteen years old. The desk was sitting under an oval window in the guest bedroom in her cabin, which she had transformed into a writing room. Outside the window, a hard wind was screaming and whining as it searched for a way into the cabin. The sound of the wind was chilling, but Sarah attempted to not let it bother her. At the age of forty-one, she knew better than to let the sound of a scary wind spook her mind. Still, she thought, running her hands through her short blond hair, there was something about a howling wind that could make a grown man cringe in fear. "You're a silly twit," Sarah told herself, and rolled her pale blue eyes at the wind. "Scream on, my friend."

Sarah stood and stretched her sore back. She examined the old blue robe she was wearing. Standing here, in a room lined with priceless hardwood flooring, walls painted soft blue and filled with beautiful art, an antique bookshelf consumed with wonderful volumes, and a smiling, warm fireplace, Sarah knew that her old robe was surely out of place. "It doesn't matter," she said aloud in a sad voice. "Who's here to see me wearing my old robe? I'm a forty-one-year-old divorced woman with no children. I'm also a retired detective hiding away in Alaska, writing silly books and running a coffee shop... Sure, bachelors are lining up at my door and begging to have a cup of coffee with me." She grinned wryly.

Sarah looked down at the computer sitting on the writing desk. The black words stood out in sharp contrast to the glowing white screen, telling of a strange, dangerous mystery. The books Sarah wrote had become a splash, and she had created a large following of readers that generously supplied her bank account with more money than she had ever dreamed of having. She had assumed she would waste her forties away working as a street detective in Los Angeles until retirement. Sarah was secretly thrilled when her publisher handed her a check with six digits and promised her more to come. Recently divorced and heartbroken, Sarah decided to take her money, retire early, and relocate to the small town she had visited with her sister the previous year. "I'm not so sure about the pen name I chose to write under, though," Sarah cautioned herself. "I've made too many enemies back in Los Angeles. And maybe it would be a good idea to take my real name out of the story and replace it with a fake one...silly me."

Realizing that she was talking to herself while standing in a lonely room, Sarah sighed. "Coffee time," she said and left her writing room.

Sarah walked into her small, cozy kitchen featuring a creamy green floor and light brown walls and paused. Her eyes went to the wooden bird clock hanging over the circular kitchen table covered with a pink-and-white tablecloth. "Not even ten in the morning," Sarah spoke into the empty kitchen. "Insomnia isn't a fair weather friend."

After making a pot of coffee, she plopped herself down at the kitchen table and tossed her eyes toward the square window standing over the kitchen sink. A heavy snow was falling, preventing any attempts to travel into town. "Plows will be by later...maybe then I'll go into town and check on the coffee shop?" Sarah said to herself. She liked her coffee shop. She liked the idea that not only was she a successful writer, but also an independent businesswoman running a successful coffee shop—well, a mediocre coffee shop. The shop was housed in an old bakery sitting at the end of a snowy street that wasn't even mentioned on most street maps. Still, it was hers, and the locals seemed to like it. "Maybe a trip into town will be nice," Sarah said, trying to escape the loneliness she was feeling.

Suddenly she was overwhelmed by a wave of memories of her ex-husband, and she had to fight back tears. "Why?" she asked heartbrokenly. Sarah recalled, as she had so many times before, the man she had been married to for twenty years walking into their home in Los Angeles and announcing that he wanted a divorce. She had been sitting in the kitchen reading a case file when he delivered this news. Shocked and unable to respond, she watched her husband walk away without saying a word—and walk right out of their marriage.

The white telephone began to ring from the living room, interrupting her thoughts. Sarah quickly wiped at a tear and stood up. She hurried into the warm, comfortable living room with walls made of old logs and a beautiful hardwood floor, sat down on the dark tan leather couch and grabbed the phone. "Hello?"

"Hey, Los Angeles," a cheery voice said, "what are you doing today?"

"Oh, hey June Bug," Sarah said. It was her friend, Amanda Funnel. Amanda had recently relocated from London to Alaska with her husband. They wanted to be close to their son, who lived in Fairbanks, forty miles south of Snow Falls.

"You're sad," Amanda said in a quick voice. "Thinking of Harry again?"

"Trying not to would be the correct response," Sarah admitted. Drawing in a deep breath, she looked at the stone fireplace across the living room. A gentle fire was nestled in the fireplace, giving off a delicate heat that warmed the room. Sitting on the mantle was a photo of Sarah and her former husband, holding hands, standing on the beach back in California. "It takes time."

"That creep isn't worth your time," Amanda told Sarah in a stern tone. "That bloke divorced you to marry a rich woman, leaving you to fend for yourself."

"I know...I know," Sarah said, fighting back more tears. "Harry left me to marry his client. I guess it's true...all lawyers are crooks." She scoffed.

"Listen," Amanda said, "I'm calling because my dear husband is flying back to London today. Lionel has become ill and Simon needs to tend to him. So, since I'm going to be alone for a week, I thought I might come and stay with you."

"You're not flying out with Simon?" Sarah asked, surprised.

"Let's just say that my father-in-law and I...were never close," Amanda admitted. "Anyway, the plows are running on my side of town. As soon as they get to you, give me a call and I'll drive over and take a holiday at your flat...just us girls...popcorn...fingernail polish..."

Sarah smiled. She loved her friend, even though she had known the woman less than a year. "Sure," she said. "No, wait, meet me in town at the coffee shop. I want to open up for a few hours and try to bring in a few bucks."

"Well, the snow is supposed to fly over us by noon. Sure, why not," Amanda agreed.

Sarah smiled again. "In this town, a woman has to open her store when the weather permits. Yesterday I got snowed in out here. If I don't open up for a few hours today, the folks in town might think I'm closing my business."

"The blokes in town will tar and feather you if you dared to try," Amanda laughed. "Now, put on a brave smile and go take a hot shower. And," she added, "get out of that old, ratty robe you're no doubt wearing at this very moment."

Sarah glanced down at her robe. "Maybe I'll change into something more appropriate," she giggled sweetly. "I'll see you in town, June Bug."

"I'll be there, Los Angeles. You just make sure that you don't stand me up," Amanda said in an affectionate voice.

Feeling better from the phone call, Sarah wandered back to the kitchen and drank a cup of coffee. By the time she had showered and changed into a thick, green sweater and jeans, she felt ready to take on the world again. "I'll tend to my coffee shop, have a bite to eat with June Bug, come back home and write some and...oh dear," Sarah hurried to her writing room. "With Amanda sleeping over, I won't have time to write, and my book is due in two months..." Biting her thumbnail, she focused on the computer sitting on her writing desk. The computer was still on. "One step at a time," she told herself and closed the door to her writing room.

She threw on a clumsy but very warm brown winter parka, then grabbed her green backpack hanging on the wooden coat rack next to the front door and slung it over her shoulder. Next, she grabbed her Subaru keys hanging from the hook next to the coat rack and braced herself to battle the icy wind and thick snow as she headed outside. Sarah spotted a large red snowplow pushing its way down her snow-covered road. She waved at the driver and then studied her driveway. "Let's get to it," she said with a deep sigh and struggled to her Subaru. After placing her backpack on the passenger's seat, she forced her way through the snow to a small utility shed on the north side of her cabin and retrieved a snow shovel. "Oh, the weather outside is tiring...so so tiring...and since I have someplace to go...let me shovel, let me shovel, let me shovel..." Sarah began singing as she started the difficult task of shoveling out her driveway.

Shovelful by shovelful, Sarah worked to clear her driveway as the icy winds clawed at her. At least the snow was letting up and the skies were turning blue, even though the temperature was well below twenty degrees. "Thanks a lot, Harry," Sarah complained after clearing her driveway and putting the snow shovel back in the utility shed. "I hope you're enjoying living in sunny California without me."

Refusing to become upset, Sarah walked to her Subaru, climbed into the driver's seat, and cautiously drove into the small town of Snow Falls. "Snow tires, don't fail me now." As she maneuvered down her snowy road, she admired the cabins that sat at comfortable distances from one another—each cabin was covered with snow and had smoke coming from its chimney. "A girl could really create some stories about this place," Sarah said. "I think I'm going to be okay in Snow Falls."

Chapter Two

Twenty minutes later, Sarah turned down a recently-plowed street lined with wooden buildings that were homes to a bakery, a small bank, a diner, a general store, a hardware store, a bookstore and video rental store, a lawyer's office, a small newspaper office, and of course, her coffee shop, which was located at the end of the street next to the hardware store and across from the bookstore. The street was white and welcoming, cozy and mysterious all at the same time—just the way Sarah liked it. Spotting Amanda's truck sitting in front of her coffee shop, she swung her Subaru into the parking space beside the truck, waved, and rolled down her window.

"Blimey, it's cold," Amanda exclaimed, getting out of her blue 1987 Chevy Silverado. Sarah smiled. Her friend looked like a polar bear, wrapped in a thick white coat large enough to cover Antarctica. Her brown hair was covered with a gray wool cap with flaps that dropped down over her ears. "Not a word," Amanda said, catching Sarah examining her appearance.

Sarah looked down at the pair of brown snow boots Amanda was wearing. "You look...chic," Sarah teased.

Amanda rolled her eyes. "I'm freezing, Los Angeles. Get me inside, quickly."

Sarah laughed. Grabbing her backpack, she carefully exited her Subaru, walked up onto an icy sidewalk that was in desperate need of being sanded, and approached her coffee shop. Before unlocking the front door, she studied the street. "Not many people are out today. I doubt I'll get any business. Most likely I'm going to waste some electricity," she said, still standing bravely against the icy winds even though her ears had begun to cry out in pain.

"I'll buy all the coffee you have, just get me inside," Amanda begged.

Sarah quickly unlocked the wooden door with the small oval window at the top and moved aside. Amanda rushed through it, nearly slipping and falling as she did. Sarah followed, pulling the door shut behind her, and reached to her right to flip on two light switches. Bright overhead lights popped on, illuminating a room lined with five square wooden tables sitting on a hardwood floor, facing five chestnut brown stools connected to a long brown marble counter. All the windows had been boarded up after a blizzard had nearly destroyed half the town. Sarah didn't mind her coffee shop being windowless—somehow, the lack of windows added a sense of mystery that she loved. And sure, the shop looked more like a place where rough lumberjacks would hang out rather than tea-drinking ladies, but that only added to the atmosphere.

Shivering, Amanda grabbed a stool and sat down. "Coffee, please," she pleaded.

"Leave me a good tip," Sarah winked as she walked behind the front counter and disappeared through the swinging door that led to the small kitchen. The kitchen held an old refrigerator, a stove that barely worked and cabinets that barely managed to hang on the walls—but Sarah loved her kitchen, as old and rundown as it was. She headed across the dark brown linoleum floor toward her office, which was nothing more than a pantry into which she had shoved a desk and computer. "Ah, the good life," Sarah said, squeezing into her office and tossing her backpack down onto the wooden desk that she had found at an antique store in Fairbanks. "Now, let's see if I can check my email, since I can't get internet service at my cabin."

Sitting down in her comfortable black computer chair, Sarah turned on the computer and methodically checked her email. After composing an email to her publisher, she took off her coat, walked back into the kitchen, and got to work making four pots of fresh, hot coffee and a batch of homemade cinnamon rolls. After a little while, Amanda joined her. "This joint has terrible service," she teased Sarah. "I've been waiting for my coffee for over twenty minutes."

Sarah pointed to the stove. "The old fashioned way takes time," she said as she stood at the wooden counter with her hands dipped into a bowl full of flour.

Amanda eased her eyes toward the kitchen door. "Say," she said in a low whisper, "actually, some bloke walked in a minute ago and sat down. I thought I should come back here and tell you."

"You didn't recognize him?" Sarah asked in a curious voice. Her friend was not the type of person to let a face pass by. Amanda Funnel knew every person in Snow Falls, and every person knew her.

Amanda shook her head no. "I'll pour myself a cup of coffee and finish up these cinnamon rolls. You'd better go play waitress."

Sarah wiped her hands on the white apron she was wearing. "I guess I'd better," she agreed.

Amanda took the apron off of Sarah. "I'll bring the coffee out when it's ready, too."

"What would I do without you?" Sarah asked Amanda in a warm voice.

"Don't ask me to leave you a tip," Amanda teased and nodded toward the kitchen door. "He's a handsome bloke," she grinned.

"Oh?" Sarah asked. She winked at Amanda. "Then let me check my hair and makeup."

"You're beautiful," Amanda promised, "now move it."

Sarah smiled and walked through the kitchen door. She looked past the front counter and saw a man sitting at the table near the back right corner of the shop. Sarah continued smiling brightly as she approached the table. "Cold day and good coffee," she said in a friendly voice. "What can I get for you?"

The man looked up at Sarah. "Just some coffee," he said in a preoccupied voice. "Better make it two. The mayor will be meeting me shortly."

"Mayor Dalton?" Sarah asked and then quickly backpedaled. "Of course, two coffees," she said. As she walked away she glanced over her shoulder. The strange man was wearing a nice gray suit. His hair was jet-black and his face spoke of intelligence and self-control, reminding Sarah of someone with military background. It was obvious the man was not a local.

"Well?" Amanda asked, still working on the cinnamon rolls.

"Two coffees...one for the stranger and one for the mayor, who he's meeting here," Sarah said in a strange voice.

"Really?" Amanda sounded fascinated. "Now who could that old custard tart be meeting?"

"I'm sure we'll find out soon enough," Sarah answered and hurried to make two cups of coffee. "Wish me luck," she said, now holding two brown coffee mugs in her hands.

"Good luck."

Sarah left the kitchen and spotted Mayor Dalton walking through the front door. "Ah, Sarah," he said in a pleased voice, "I'm glad you're here."

"Where else would I be?" Sarah asked in an amused voice. She liked Mayor Dalton. The man was in his late fifties, short, plump, and yes, bald. He had a delightful sense of humor and never a cruel word to say about anyone. Although Sarah noticed some people might have cruel words to say about the brown-and-green plaid suit the man was wearing.

"Of course." Mayor Dalton smiled and looked at the strange man. "Detective Conrad Spencer, I'm so glad you could make it."

"Detective?" Sarah asked, surprised.

Mayor Dalton smiled, took the two coffee mugs from Sarah's hands, and asked her to sit down with him. Sarah did as asked. She felt the writer in her secretly begin to take notes. "Detective Spencer has come to us from New York," Mayor Dalton explained, setting down the coffee mugs.

"Really?" Sarah was intrigued. "Detective Spencer, why would you leave New York to move to Snow Falls?"

"Why did you leave Los Angeles to move here? And please, call me Conrad," the detective told Sarah in a voice that was neither friendly nor hostile. He picked up one of the coffee mugs and took a sip. "So this is the woman?"

Mayor Dalton nodded his head, looking anxious. "Ms. Garland will be your go-to woman if you ever need her. Her years of experience in the field of law enforcement—"

"What are you talking about?" Sarah interrupted.

"I'm the new detective in town," Conrad told Sarah. "Mayor Dalton insisted I meet you."

"Our police department is so small, Sarah," Mayor Dalton explained nervously, "I thought it best to introduce Detective Spencer to you in case he might need—"

Sarah couldn't help but laugh. "Mayor Dalton, I'm flattered, I really am. But honestly, the only thing Detective Spencer is going to need my help with is locating a good set of snow chains. Snow Falls isn't exactly a crime-consumed metropolis."

Conrad studied Sarah's beautiful face. "I didn't think meeting you would hurt my pride," he told Sarah. "Your reputation is impressive. You've cracked some pretty tough cases back in Los Angeles."

"Detective," Sarah said, standing up, "my days of being a Dick Tracy are over. Please, excuse me."

And with that, she vanished back into the kitchen. Insulted, Conrad excused himself and left the mayor sitting alone. "Oh dear," Mayor Dalton said and began drinking his coffee.

"Well?" Amanda asked anxiously.

Sarah laughed. "It was nothing. I'll explain later. Right now, let's work on those cinnamon rolls. If we don't sell them, we can't go home."

"Good enough," Amanda said without being pushy. She knew Sarah would spill the beans when the time was right.

Chapter Three

Later, after serving only four customers and selling only two cinnamon rolls, Sarah locked up her coffee shop and drove home just as the sun was beginning to set. Amanda carefully followed in her truck. When Sarah reached her cabin, she looked into her front yard and suddenly slammed on the brakes, nearly sliding off the road. There, standing in the middle of the front yard, stood a hideous snowman wearing a black leather jacket with a candy cane shoved in its mouth. Feeling her blood turn cold, Sarah froze, unable to take her eyes off the snowman.

Amanda jumped from her truck and ran to Sarah. "What's wrong?" she asked, yanking the driver's side door open.

Sarah couldn't answer. Her eyes were locked on the snowman. The darkening sky was bathing the snowman with eerie, dangerous shadows that made it seem somehow...alive. "Sarah...hello... Hey, Los Angeles, speak to me!" Amanda said in a worried voice and began snapping her fingers in front of Sarah's face.

"How?" Sarah whispered.

"How what?" Amanda asked.

Sarah lifted a shaky finger and pointed at the snowman as the icy winds reached through the opened driver's door and snatched at her face with cruel fingers. "That..."

Amanda turned around and looked at the snowman. "The snowman?"

Sarah nodded her head. "Amanda... I didn't build that snowman... I..."

Amanda looked at Sarah and then refocused her attention back on the snowman. "What are you trying to tell me?" she asked worriedly.

Sarah forced her eyes away from the gruesome snowman and looked up at Amanda. "I need to get inside. Hurry," she said, "get back to your truck."

Amanda backed away from Sarah's Subaru. She watched Sarah back up and swing her vehicle into the driveway, get out, and make a mad dash toward her cabin. "Maybe it's the cold?" she said, confused, and got back into her truck. After parking behind the Subaru, she hurried into the cabin and found Sarah in her writing room. "Sarah?"

Sarah was sitting at her desk, staring at the computer screen. The words, "The weather outside is frightful" were written across the screen over and over and over. "No..." Sarah whispered as fear gripped her chest, "it can't be."

"What can't be?" Amanda asked, alarmed.

Sarah didn't answer. Outside, the icy winds continued to

howl and scream, and night slowly pulled the remaining light away into a cold darkness.

· ᵇ ꜟᴅ · ᵇ ꜟᴅ · ᵇ ꜟᴅ · ᵇ ꜟᴅ

As she sipped on a hot cup of coffee, Sarah struggled to control her fear. After checking her cabin for signs of illegal entry, she had found that the window to her writing room had been pried open and there was a trail of wet footprints around the writing desk; the rest of the cabin seemed untouched. "What is this all about?" Amanda asked. She was sitting at the kitchen table across from Sarah.

"Amanda, can I confide in you a very close secret that no one can ever know?" Sarah asked.

Amanda wrapped her hands around her warm cup of hot cocoa and glanced down at the Glock 19 sitting on the kitchen table in front of Sarah. "I do hate those nasty things."

"So do I, but without them, the criminals would have complete control," Sarah replied.

"True," Amanda agreed. "Okay, Los Angeles," she said, taking a deep breath, "confide away. My ears are all yours."

Sarah braced herself. She truly felt that Amanda had become more than a friend—more like a sister, she told herself. And even though trust was an issue with her, she felt that trusting Amanda seemed right. "Are you aware of the 'The Snowman Killer from Frostworth' series?"

"Los Angeles, I'm more of a 'The Happy Bunnies Take a Picnic' type woman. Now, Jack, that silly bloke, he's the one who reads those awful murder mystery books."

"Has he read the series I just mentioned?" Sarah asked.

🔴 21 🔴

Amanda frowned. "I'm afraid so," she confessed. "Whoever Milly Stevens is, she's one woman that needs a good swift kick in the pants. Jack spends his time before bed reading her books instead of talking with me."

Sarah folded her hands together and touched her mouth. "June Bug...my friend...I'm Milly Stevens. I write the 'The Snowman Killer from Frostworth' series. Milly Stevens is my pen name."

Amanda couldn't believe her ears. "No way!" she exclaimed. "You're the mental custard that's been causing my Jack to ignore me?"

Sarah winced and shrugged her shoulders. "Do you want to get me sized for a straightjacket now or wait until later?"

Amanda leaned back in her chair. "You're serious aren't you? And—" she stopped talking as a cold chill gripped her spine. "Wait a minute...oh my goodness... The front cover of the book Jack is reading has—"

"A hideous snowman wearing a leather jacket," Sarah finished.

Amanda's eyes grew large. "I just now remembered..."

"Someone built that hideous snowman in my front yard, broke into my writing room, and left me a message on my computer," Sarah explained in a calm but tense voice. "Amanda, someone is playing the part of the Frostworth Killer...and that someone knows that Milly Stevens is me."

Amanda looked toward the back door. A kitchen chair was jammed under the doorknob. "Have you got another gun?" she asked.

Sarah reached down to her ankle and took a 9mm Luger

from an ankle holster. She placed the gun down on the table and slid it across to Amanda. "Here you go."

"Sorry, Los Angeles, I might end up shooting my foot off," Amanda explained. "I didn't really think you had another gun."

Sarah left the Luger alone. "Amanda, I worked as a detective in Los Angeles for ten years. I became a cop when I was twenty-two and made detective when I was twenty-seven. During that time, I investigated some horrible crimes and tangled with some pretty bad people. Whoever built that snowman is someone who wants to mess with me, for whatever reason. And whoever that person is obviously knows that I write under the name Milly Stevens."

"You should call the police," Amanda said.

Sarah bit down on her lower lip. Then, reluctantly, she shook her head no. "Let's face it, June Bug, our local police department consists of a Chief of Police whose gun is dustier than the Sahara Desert and a few Barney Fifes that sit around at the bakery eating donuts. I like Andrew, Tom, and Edwin, but those guys couldn't track down a wounded moose if it was sleeping in front of the courthouse."

Amanda shifted her eyes to the window over the kitchen sink. Sarah had pulled the blue curtain hanging over the window closed. "What do you suggest we do, then?" she asked. "Los Angeles, someone broke into your cabin. That nasty criminal might be out there in the dark right now, watching your cabin, for all we know."

"Not in this cold. The temperature is well below zero by now. Whoever the intruder is, no one can survive outside in these temperatures."

"Hey," Amanda said in a quick, urgent voice, "you never told me about the mystery man at the coffee shop. Maybe it's him!"

"Detective Conrad Spencer from New York is our mystery man," Sarah explained. "He's the new brain in town that will be solving the case of whoever is knocking over the 'Moose Crossing' signs in town. But then again," she added, "the man sure did seem to know who I was, now didn't he?"

"He did?" Amanda asked, finally looking away from the kitchen window. "Spill the sauce, sister. I'm sitting here scared half out of my wits. This isn't no time to play 'Sherlock Holmes Loses His Memory' with me."

Sarah sipped on her coffee while organizing her thoughts. "He told me my reputation was impressive and that I had cracked some tough cases, which means he's looked into my background. But why?"

"I may be a silly Brit who isn't accustomed to your way of thinking, but I know enough to ask you to give more detail than that, please," Amanda pleaded with Sarah.

"Detective Spencer looked into my background," Sarah explained. "But why would he do that? And why would a detective from New York relocate to Snow Falls, Alaska in the first place?"

"Maybe he likes the snow?" Amanda suggested and took a sip of her hot cocoa.

"And maybe he likes building creepy snowmen?" Sarah suggested in turn.

Amanda looked across the table at her friend. "A stranger arrives in town, some bloke who seems to know about you, and all of a sudden your home is broken into and a creepy snow sculpture is left for you on your front lawn...two plus two is four, Los Angeles. I'm calling Barney Fife."

"I suppose I do need to file a report," Sarah agreed. "Sure, go ahead and call the police station."

Amanda reached across the table and patted Sarah's hand. "I'm right here with you. I'm not going anywhere. You and I are like custard and cream now, Los Angeles."

Sarah gave Amanda a grateful look. "I can see that, now. But," she said, still worried, "sometimes being the friend of a woman who has enemies can be very dangerous."

Amanda wrinkled her nose. "The British people know and understand that loyalty to duty outweighs concern for personal safety."

Sarah smiled, proud to have such a supportive friend. "I'll refill our hot cocoas, you call Barney Fife," she said.

Chapter Four

An hour later, a tall, thin man in uniform walked into Sarah's kitchen wearing a thick black jacket and warm ski cap pulled down over his ears. He greeted Sarah and Amanda, removing the gray winter hat from his head, and closed the kitchen door. "Ladies, sorry I'm late. The roads are icy tonight, can't go over fifteen or twenty miles per hour out there."

Amanda couldn't help but grin. Andrew Mayfield looked as silly as he did cold. He reminded her of a clown she had seen at a circus once. Yet there was a sweetness to his face that was honest and sincere. Sure, the man wasn't a combat warrior, but at least he was someone whose heart was warm. "Coffee?" she asked.

Andrew quickly nodded. "That would be great, thanks. And while we're at it, you'd better make a second cup for Detective Spencer. He was right behind me."

"Detective Spencer?" Sarah asked, alarmed.

"Yep. He was with me at the station when your call came

through," Andrew explained. He became very solemn. "All of us guys aren't sure about him. He's a strange sort of type... neither black nor white...just gray and cold."

"I see," Sarah said uneasily and glanced at Amanda. "Two cups of coffee, governor," she said in a pitiful, nervous British accent.

Amanda bit down on her lower lip and looked at the back door. "Sure, two cups of coffee, love," she answered back.

Andrew began twiddling with his hat. "Us guys, we're all wondering why a man like Detective Spencer would leave New York and move all the way up here to Alaska. He doesn't have any family in this part of the world...doesn't make a bit of sense to anyone."

"And the pay cut from New York to Alaska must have been harsh, too," Sarah added. "Any idea where the new detective is residing, Andrew?"

"Over on Polar Bear Lane. He's rented a room from Old Lady Grizzly herself," Andrew informed her. "What a pair, you know?"

Sarah didn't immediately respond. Her mind was struggling to make sense of Conrad Spencer. "Okay, thanks, Andrew. Please, sit down."

Andrew shook his head no. "I'd rather stand and—" A hard knock on the back door silenced Andrew in mid-sentence. "It's him," he whispered.

Amanda walked to the kitchen table and set down two cups of coffee. Sarah had the Luger resting in her ankle holster and her Glock at the ready, hidden under her purse next to the coffee pot. Amanda watched as Sarah made her way over to the kitchen counter and inched her hand closer to her purse. "Open the door," Sarah told Andrew in a controlled but worried voice.

Andrew turned around and opened the back door. A dark figure appeared, stepped across the threshold and pushed the back door shut with his black snow boot. Amanda hurried over to Sarah and grabbed her hand in fright. The man standing before them was wearing a black ski mask and a thick, black coat...and he was carrying a gun. "Detective," Andrew said in a polite voice, "thought you got lost there for a bit."

Conrad took his left hand and removed the ski mask from his face, revealing a human being rather than a monster. "Have you looked around?" he asked Andrew in a stern tone.

"Not yet," Andrew answered. "I wanted to wait for you."

"Good," Conrad said and focused his attention on Sarah. "When did you notice the unlawful intrusion?" he asked.

"Are you hunting for night owls?" Sarah asked instead, nodding her head at the gun Conrad was holding in his right hand.

Conrad looked down at his gun. "You know our business," he scolded Sarah. "The intruder who broke into your home could still be lurking around. On a night like this, we're the hunted and he is the hunter."

"Nobody is lurking around outside in this cold," Andrew assured Conrad. "Detective Spencer, you're not a native of these parts, so let me put your mind at ease when I tell you that no man can survive in these temperatures."

"Maybe," Conrad agreed. He shivered, feeling frozen to the core. Hesitantly, he removed his coat and placed it on the wooden coat rack next to the back door and then stuffed his gun into a brown leather shoulder holster. "Let's take a look at the window."

"Just a minute," Sarah said. Keeping her hand close to her purse, she studied Conrad's face. "Do you mind me asking why you looked into my background? I'm the type of woman who becomes curious when a stranger knows about her past."

Conrad folded his arms and locked eyes with Sarah. "The mayor mentioned you to me. Your name sounded familiar. When I finally remembered who you were, I ran your name. Two years before you left Los Angeles, you and I were working on the same case, but thousands of miles apart."

"Were we?" Sarah asked curiously.

"Yes, we were," Conrad answered in a strict tone. "We were both working to take down the 'Alley Man.' And if you remember, there was an 'Alley Man' copycat. New York and Los Angeles weren't sure which city was housing the real killer and—"

"And I took down the real killer," Sarah finished.

"And I tackled the copycat," Conrad finished. "When the mayor mentioned your name, a bell went off in my head. I could hardly believe the same woman who took down the 'Alley Man' killer was living in the same town I was relocating to."

"Why did you come to Snow Falls, by the way?" Sarah asked carefully. She began to think back to the 'Alley Man' case. Could Conrad Spencer be the 'Alley Man' copycat, pretending to be a detective?

Conrad rubbed his forehead and looked at Sarah, then at Andrew, and then to Amanda. "I know that people are curious. I would be, too, if a stranger from New York moved way out here to this glacier." Reaching into his back pocket, Conrad pulled out a black wallet, opened it, and retrieved a photo of a beautiful woman with bright blond hair. He walked over to Sarah and handed her the photo. "This is a photo of my ex-wife."

"She's very pretty," Sarah replied, examining the photo.

"Very pretty, indeed," Amanda agreed. Andrew watched with curious eyes.

"She was placed in the witness protection program... I can't say any more than that," Conrad explained and took the photo back from Sarah. "My ex-wife and I weren't close...messy divorce...hard words...angry feelings..." Conrad shook his head.

"Was your ex-wife brought here to Snow Falls?" Amanda asked Conrad.

Conrad nodded. "You wouldn't have recognized her, though. She colored her hair black and cut it short and began wearing glasses. She also deliberately put on weight."

"The Mafia or something was after her, is that it?" Sarah asked.

Conrad didn't answer, but his eyes told Sarah the truth. "My ex-wife was found frozen...to death...last month."

Sarah looked at Andrew. Andrew glanced away and kicked at his feet. "I guess it makes sense now," he said.

"You know about his ex-wife?" Amanda asked Andrew in shock.

"The chief was ordered by higher-ups to keep the death of that poor lady quiet," Andrew explained. "Detective, I had no idea that woman was your wife."

"It's all right," Conrad told Andrew. "I'm only here

looking for the person who killed my wife and then I'm going back to New York. It may just be coincidence, but—" he said, and then stopped, focusing on Sarah.

"But what?" Sarah asked.

"I could use your help," Conrad admitted. "Los Angeles wasn't very happy to see you leave to come up here and play with the polar bears."

"I had my reasons," Sarah told Conrad. She read sadness in his tough, stern eyes. To avoid further requests for help, Sarah stood and said abruptly, "This way, Detective. Amanda, stay in the kitchen with Andrew, okay?"

"Sure, love," Amanda promised.

Sarah walked Conrad to her writing room. Conrad methodically examined every inch of the room as the icy winds screamed and howled outside. "No wet footprints outside the range of the writing desk?"

"No," Sarah replied and pointed at the window. "Crowbar was used to pry the window open."

Conrad examined the window. He pulled back the curtains and used his fingers to feel the wood the crowbar had damaged. "Do you have any enemies in this town?" he asked, lifting his fingers and peering into the dark night.

"I may make lousy coffee, but most people in this town like me," Sarah explained.

"Sure," Conrad said, choosing to ignore Sarah's self-deprecating joke. "Did you check outside for footprints?"

Sarah shook her head no. "Wind took the prints away long before I got home."

Conrad walked away from the window, sat down on the

edge of the writing desk, and folded his arms. "Talk to me, Detective Garland."

"I'm retired," Sarah reminded him. She sat down in the computer chair and focused on the computer. "These words were left for me as a message."

Conrad looked down and read the words sneering up at him from the computer screen. "Any ideas?"

"Some," Sarah admitted, bringing her hands to her eyes and rubbing them. "But first, you move your pawn and let's see where we're at."

"Okay, Milly Stevens," Conrad said in an even voice.

Sarah sighed miserably. "You have conducted your research, haven't you?"

"Female cop moves to the same town my ex-wife was found dead outside of...same female cop who tackled the 'Alley Man'...makes a man suspicious," Conrad said. He tossed off his gloves as if preparing to go toe-to-toe with Sarah. "Why did you really move here, Detective? You could write your books anywhere. Who are you after? Are you after the same people I'm tailing? Talk to me, okay? We're both on the same team, here."

"Are we?" Sarah asked and stood up. "Detective Spencer—"

"Conrad."

"Sure, fine, Conrad...my husband left me for a very wealthy client. He broke my heart into a million little pieces. I..." Sarah ran her hands through her blond hair. "I couldn't stay in Los Angeles anymore. I needed to begin a new life for myself."

"Why did you choose to begin that new life in Snow Falls, Alaska?"

"I have always loved Alaska—the land, the people, the snow...not so much the cold, though," Sarah explained. "My book series is doing very well. I am in a position, financially, to be able to write my books full time."

"Why did you start a coffee shop, then?"

"My papa," Sarah said. She walked to the window. Outside, a thick, frozen darkness glared at her. "My papa owned a coffee shop when I was a little girl, when we lived in Wisconsin. I have fond memories of Papa's coffee shop. I suppose I...owning my coffee shop makes me feel close to Papa. After losing my husband, I needed an anchor, okay?"

"Good enough," Conrad said. He politely backed off the topic and created a different path to walk down. "Could be the man who killed my ex-wife found out your identity and now he's after you?"

"You haven't read my books, have you?" Sarah asked Conrad, turning away from the dark window.

"Not really, no," Conrad admitted.

"You can't see it, but there's a snowman standing out on my front lawn wearing a black leather jacket," Sarah explained. "In my book, the killer leaves the same kind of snowman on the front lawn of his intended victims. Someone in this town knows that I'm Milly Stevens."

Conrad rubbed his chin. "It took some digging on my part to find out your pen name. Whoever this person is must have some contacts. Your publisher keeps your true identity extremely secure."

"How did you find out that I write under the name of Milly Stevens, then?" Sarah insisted.

"Your ex-husband," Conrad told her in a matter-of-fact voice. "The guy told me you moved away somewhere to write stories. I did some additional exploring and talked to some of the guys in Los Angeles. I was told by a Sergeant Lucas that you had a book published before you dropped your shield in the trash."

"I didn't drop my shield in the trash," Sarah snapped. "Oh, Lucas...she always had a big mouth. She was always snooping around my desk, too. I can't tell you how many times I had to run her off."

"This Sergeant Lucas dreams of being the next Sherlock Holmes," Conrad said sympathetically. "She seemed very bitter toward you, by the way."

"Our last encounter wasn't very pleasant," Sarah confessed. "My husband and I were going through the divorce and I found her sitting at my desk reading a letter my publisher had sent me. I scolded her pretty well...and embarrassed her in front of a lot of people. Oh, it was stupid of me to leave that letter on my desk. My mind was... I was upset and wasn't thinking clearly, that's all."

"I understand," Conrad said in a voice that had warmed up one degree. "So," he said, rubbing his nose, "someone in Snow Falls knows that you are Milly Stevens and left you a message out on your front lawn as well as on your computer."

"Which means that person will return for me...eventually. First, he...or she...will play the game of the Frostworth Killer."

"Frostworth?" he asked, curiously.

"A fictional town," Sarah explained. Her eyes focused on her writing desk, and she saw herself sitting in the computer chair for countless hours as her fingertips created one word after another, each word connecting and forming a mystery story about a dangerous killer. "I suppose I have my career as a homicide detective to thank for the idea."

Conrad studied Sarah's writing room. The room was warm and inviting—yet, mysterious. The woman herself, Conrad noticed, was mysterious...and extremely beautiful. He found it hard not to stare at Sarah's face. "Do you miss your shield?" he dared to ask.

"At times," Sarah admitted, "and at other times I'm grateful to be rid of my shield. A lot of baggage comes with being a homicide detective...but you know that."

Conrad nodded. "Currently I have insomnia," he said and smiled miserably. "It happens."

Sarah looked deeply into Conrad's eyes. "I have insomnia, too. Not bad...but I'm only catching four hours of sleep a night."

"Better than my three," Conrad replied. "I started losing sleep about six months ago, right out of the blue. I started waking up earlier and earlier, which is unusual because I can usually sleep twelve hours straight."

Even though Sarah was exhausted, scared, and worried by the situation, somehow standing in her writing room with Conrad gave her a strange sense of comfort. "My insomnia began about four months back. I was never a heavy sleeper; eight hours and I'm up. I...I began losing sleep when I started writing the third book to the 'The Snowman Killer from Frostworth' series."

Conrad glanced at the dark window. Suddenly he stood up, walked over to the window and pulled the curtains closed. "Let's get back to the kitchen."

Sarah nodded. As she closed the door to her writing room after Conrad, she felt a cold chill. Her instinct told her that she was now the main character in her book, and that whoever was after her meant to end the final sentence without a happy ending.

Chapter Five

"Everything all right?" Amanda asked as the detective and ex-detective reentered the room. Sitting at the kitchen table with Andrew, she felt somewhat safe—but still very scared.

"A crowbar was used to pry the window open," Conrad told Andrew. "Check with the local hardware store to see if anyone has purchased a crowbar in the last few days. Also, check with the hotel. I want the names of all the guests."

Andrew laughed so hard coffee nearly came out of his nose. "Sorry..." he said, raising a hand to Conrad, "but the only guest the Moose Inn has this time of year is a bear or two snuggled up outside one of the rooms."

"Check," Conrad ordered Andrew.

Andrew shrugged his shoulders. "You're the boss," he said in a calm voice, "but Detective Spencer, Snow Falls has a population of twenty-four thousand people, mostly seasonal folks who leave when winter arrives. Sure, we have a large department store and a couple of fast food places sitting on the south side of town, and maybe our Main Street looks like it's growing—"

"It does?" Amanda asked skeptically.

"Well, maybe Main Street isn't booming," Andrew corrected himself. "My point is, when winter arrives, Snow Falls shuts down. Tourists flock to Fairbanks and Anchorage."

Conrad walked to the kitchen table and slammed down his fist hard, scaring Amanda. "Someone in this town killed my ex-wife. Someone in this town broke into this cabin. Do I make myself clear?" he asked Andrew.

Andrew looked up into a pair of angry eyes. "Sure, Detective, you make yourself clear," he said and stood up. "I guess I'd better get back to the station and file a report on the break-in."

Conrad closed his eyes and shook his head. He reached out his hand and touched Andrew's shoulder. "Hey, I'm sorry. I didn't mean to snap like that. We have to be careful, that's all. Where I come from, a killer plays outside the rules of the game."

"Detective Spencer is right," Sarah told Andrew. "Whoever broke into my cabin intends on playing a very dangerous game with me that doesn't end well for the hero. And whoever killed Detective Spencer's wife isn't someone who isn't just going away."

"Sure, I get it," Andrew said, "but two killers...right here in Snow Falls...that's kinda hard to swallow."

"I'm not implying the man who killed my ex-wife is still hanging around drinking coffee," Conrad told Andrew in a controlled voice. "I'm here looking for answers, okay? Now, drive back to the station and file your report and keep quiet. Don't tell anyone what we've talked about here tonight, are we clear?"

"Not even the guys?"

"No one," Conrad ordered.

"The guys are really going to rag me about this," Andrew said in an upset voice.

"No one," Conrad reiterated firmly.

Andrew sighed. "You sure are making life rough for me," he told Conrad as he put on his winter hat. "Sarah, keep your doors locked."

"I will, trust me. You just be careful driving back into town," Sarah replied worriedly. "Do you want a coffee to go?"

"Thanks, but no," Andrew said, grateful that Sarah was worried about him. "Heather has made me promise to cut down to three cups a night. Bye, now."

Sarah watched Andrew leave. Amanda stood up and maneuvered her way toward the coffee pot. "A coffee to go?" she asked Conrad.

Conrad shook his head no. "I've had enough coffee for today, thank you." Conrad retrieved his coat, put it on deliberately, and then donned the black ski mask. "Detective Garland, you be careful tonight," he said, and then he vanished into the cold, icy night.

"Well?" Amanda asked in an urgent voice. "Is he the one?"

Sarah rubbed her neck. "I'm afraid not. Detective Spencer is on the up and up."

Amanda frowned. "Does he have any idea who broke into your cabin?" she asked.

"No," Sarah said in a concerned voice. Leaning back against the kitchen counter, she studied the back door. "But no one is out there tonight except for that creepy snowman. The wind is actually working as our defender tonight. I think we're safe."

Amanda wasn't so sure. She hugged her arms and looked at the back door too. "Silly Jack, he did have to leave town, didn't he? Perhaps it wasn't such a bright idea to remain behind."

Sarah wrapped her arm around Amanda. "June Bug, I'm sure glad that you did stay behind. I need you."

Outside in the darkness, Conrad watched Andrew cautiously move up the street and away from the cabin. As Andrew disappeared from sight, Conrad moved into Sarah's front yard. In the distance, he saw a shadowy figure that seemed to be waving at him. Drawing out his gun, he eased toward the figure as his eyes searched the darkness and howling winds. If someone was daring enough to brave the frigid temperatures, he certainly couldn't see that person yet. The only light emanating into the snowy darkness was from the cabin— everything else was complete and utter darkness. "Careful now," he said in a whisper as he approached the hideous snowman.

With his gun at the ready, Conrad leaned forward and examined what he could see of the snowman. The cabin's living room window cast enough light onto the snowy figure to illuminate its face in an eerie glow. Biting down on his lower lip, Conrad reached out his left hand and felt the leather jacket. The leather was new. Nodding his head, he snatched the jacket off the snowman and backed away toward the cabin, staring at the candy cane sticking out of the snowman's mouth. It was obvious the mafia had sent a hit man to kill his ex-wife—but no mafia stooge had left a deadly message for Sarah in the form of a creepy snowman chewing on a candy cane. Whoever had built the snowman was someone who had a personal vendetta against a woman who wrote under the pen name of Milly Stevens. "I'd better keep my eyes on Sarah," Conrad whispered to himself, and he carefully walked back to the green truck he had purchased in Fairbanks.

Chapter Six

Back in town, Conrad walked into a medium-sized wooden building that appeared to be more of a log cabin than a police station. Soaking in the heat coming from both the overhead ceiling vents and the floor vents, he walked across a small lobby that resembled a coffee shop and into the work area of the station, which was nothing more than a square area lined with four desks. Snatching off his ski mask, Conrad looked down at the glossy hardwood floor and nodded his head; at least the police station was spotlessly clean, which he liked. He stopped at Andrew's desk, where Andrew was currently sitting, hunt-and-pecking away at his keyboard. "Check with the department store in town and see if this leather jacket was purchased there," he instructed, tossing the jacket that had been on the snowman down onto Andrew's desk.

Andrew looked at the leather jacket. "Yep," he said in a quick voice, "I can tell you right now that jacket was bought at Old Man O'Mally's store."

"How?" Conrad demanded. He sat down on the edge of Andrew's desk.

Andrew gathered the jacket into his hands and examined the material. "Because my wife bought me one just like it for my birthday two weeks ago," he told Conrad. "Not a bad jacket, but leather isn't my style... And look here," he added, showing Conrad an inside clothing tag, "see that 'M' written in green marker? Old Man O'Mally always marks his clothes like that. He's a bit paranoid, if you catch my drift."

Conrad was gaining a new respect for this small town cop who he'd been sure was incapable of driving in the snow just a few hours ago. "Okay, Andrew, this is between you and me. I took this jacket off a weird-looking snowman someone had built in the front yard of Sarah Garland's cabin. It's likely the person who built the snowman is the same person who broke into her cabin. Now, here is where it gets interesting... Sarah Garland is writing a mystery series. In the series, there's a killer who leaves the same kind of creepy snowman I found tonight on the front lawns of his intended victims. I'm guessing the leather jacket is an added accessory to the message left for the intended victim."

Andrew listened calmly. He slowly folded his arms across his chest and nodded. "Someone wants to kill Sarah?"

"Seems to be that way. Sarah... Detective Garland may have made an enemy or two back in Los Angeles working as a homicide detective."

"But Sarah...she's never bothered a soul," Andrew said. "Sure, her coffee isn't the greatest in town—heck, you can get better coffee down at the filling station, but that's no reason to want to harm her."

"Someone in Snow Falls is out to harm her and it's our job to find out who, Andrew. I'm going to need your help on this case, okay?"

"Sure, I'll do all that I can," Andrew promised.

Conrad studied the leather jacket again. "No one is to know about this case, are we clear? I know you and the other guys are close pals, and that's fine. But right now I need closed mouths."

"Sure, I understand," Andrew agreed. "The guys and me, we do tend to be long-winded at times. But you have to understand, we're a tight family around here, Detective Spencer. Snow Falls isn't just another town; it's a home where people live together, laugh together, cry together...survive together. In Snow Falls, everyone is family. When Sarah arrived, it didn't take any time at all for us to bring her into our group and welcome her as one of our own. That's the way we are in Snow Falls. The guys find out I'm keeping something from them—and they will—they're going to give me an awfully hard time. But I'll do what you asked me to, for Sarah."

Conrad reached out and patted Andrew's shoulder. "I'm grateful," he said. "I can see that I'm putting you in a tight spot. I guess everyone will be glad when I leave and some local guy comes in that fits in better," he added ruefully.

Andrew studied Conrad's face. He saw a man who appeared to be very tired and very hurt inside. "I'm awful sorry about your ex-wife. You must have still cared about her if you came all this way to find the person who killed her."

Conrad folded his arms together. "She was a feisty Italian who had a sassy mouth and a red-hot temper. Her brother was what people call a 'good fella'...very dangerous man. I was working undercover when I met her. She was something." Conrad smiled. "I had never met anyone like her. Before I knew it, I was hooked on her and she was hooked on me. I knew better, but...well, I married her. But when she found out I was an undercover cop...the fireworks started."

"I bet," Andrew said.

Conrad nodded. "My ex-wife threatened to blow my cover, which forced me to turn in all the evidence I had against her brother. The FBI made some arrests and my ex-wife was placed into protective custody because the mob family thought she was involved with the police. By then, it was too late, though...she filed for divorce and let me know that if I ever came near her again she would happily cut my ears off."

"Ouch," Andrew said sympathetically.

Conrad closed his eyes and saw a beautiful black-haired Italian beauty. "I'm here, Andrew, because I'm responsible for her death. If I hadn't married her...she would still be alive. I owe it to my ex-wife to find out who killed her."

Andrew stood up and patted Conrad's shoulder. "You have a friend on your side," he promised.

"I know," Conrad said gratefully. He stood up and walked back toward the small office that had been assigned to him, and then paused. He turned around and looked at Andrew. "There is a killer loose in Snow Falls, Andrew. This person is after Sarah Garland, but he may not stop with her. I need you to understand how deadly this situation is."

Andrew suddenly felt a cold chill grab him—colder than

the air outside. "Detective," he said, "maybe it wouldn't be a bad idea if we brought Sarah into town, for her own protection."

Conrad shook his head no. "Sarah Garland isn't going to run scared," he replied and walked away.

Outside, the icy winds screamed as a light snow began to fall. Far away, tucked into a small rental cabin, a pair of hands held up a photo of Sarah Garland wearing her police uniform. "Oh, the weather outside is frightful..." the voice began to sing, and then laughed.

Chapter Seven

Sarah stifled a yawn and rubbed her eyes as she brought the coffee pot to life. The pot slowly gurgled and wafted the smell of delicious coffee into the warm kitchen air. "Hurry up," Sarah pleaded with the coffee pot. She walked to the kitchen table with her gun in hand. After only managing to capture four hours of sleep, she felt horrible. "Hurry up, coffee, please."

"Morning," Amanda said, stumbling into the kitchen with her hair in a mess. Spotting the coffee pot, she smiled and then yawned. "You're already dressed," she observed in a not-so-surprised voice.

Sarah looked down at her gun sitting on the table. "I'm up," she replied and slowly began straightening a few wrinkles out of the gray flannel shirt she was wearing with her tired hands. The shirt was warm and protective against the cold, even though it was bland and not very stylish. Sarah wasn't interested in style, though—she was interested in tracking down a dangerous criminal. "You'd better get dressed, too," she told Amanda, shaking her head at the pink bunny slippers Amanda was wearing.

Amanda looked down at the pink pajamas she was wearing and then focused on her bunny slippers. "What do you say, love?" she asked the bunny slippers, "should we get dressed or lounge around in this cabin all day? What's that?... Oh, okay, we'll get dressed."

Sarah smiled. Amanda's silliness always seemed to cheer her up. "It's snowing outside. I was thinking that we could drive into town in my Subaru and leave your truck here."

"Ah, the old 'leave the second vehicle at home' to make it appear that, well, someone is home," Amanda said, pretending to speak in a brilliant voice.

"Wouldn't hurt," Sarah protested. "The truth is, whoever built that snowman and broke into my writing room might be watching the cabin right now. Who knows?"

Amanda walked to the kitchen table and sat down across from Sarah. "And why are we driving into town, love?" she asked curiously.

"I noticed the snowman's leather jacket was missing. I called the police station and was able to get a contact number for Detective Spencer," Sarah explained. "I called him."

"He took the jacket?"

"Yes." Sarah looked at the coffee pot. "He wants to meet at the coffee shop in about two hours. Poor guy has insomnia like I do. He had only been asleep for two hours when I woke him up. I hope he was able to catch a few more winks."

"Who says cops are morning people?" Amanda teased Sarah.

"Not me... I would give anything to get a regular eight

hours of sleep," Sarah sighed. She had just stood up when a hard *thump* struck the back door. Falling into police mode, Sarah grabbed her gun and dropped down to one knee, aiming at the back door. Amanda scrambled down onto the floor and crawled behind Sarah for protection. A second *thump* struck the back door. "Sounds like rocks," Sarah whispered.

"If you say so," Amanda said in a scared voice.

Sarah waited and listened. Silence fell. No more 'thumps' arrived. "Wait here," she told Amanda and duck-walked to the back door. Drawing in a deep breath, she reached up, unlocked the door handle, and cautiously eased the back door open just far enough to see outside. Vicious winds and heavy snow greeted her. Her eyes darted over the backyard, searching for boot tracks. "There," Sarah said, spotting a set of boot tracks leading into the woods. Looking down, she saw two rocks surrounded by crumpled snow that appeared to have formed snowballs around them.

"Well?" Amanda asked from a safe distance.

Sarah closed the back door, locked it, and duck-walked back to Amanda. "Rocks inside snowballs," she explained, "and boot prints leading into the woods."

"What do we do?" Amanda asked, grabbing Sarah's arm.

"Photos," Sarah said quickly and stood up. She ran to the kitchen counter, put her gun down and grabbed her purse. "Cell phone..."

Amanda watched Sarah dig out a cell phone from her purse, grab her gun, and run to the back door. "What are you doing?"

"I need photos of the boot prints before the wind takes

them," Sarah explained. With her gun at the ready, she snatched open the front door and dashed outside.

"Oh dear," Amanda said, terrified. Scrambling to her feet, she looked around, saw a broom, grabbed it and then hurried out into the snow to protect her friend. "I'll protect you!" she yelled at Sarah over the screaming wind, holding the broom in her hands like a baseball bat.

"You'll freeze, get back inside," Sarah ordered. When she arrived at the set of first boot prints, she looked behind her at Amanda. Amanda, still in her bunny slippers, pushed through the snow toward her. "So stubborn," Sarah said over the wind. "Here, hold my gun...the safety is off, so if you see anyone, aim and fire."

Amanda hesitantly took Sarah's gun as the snow and wind began tearing into her frail body and feet. "Hurry," she begged Sarah.

Sarah nodded and began taking photos of the boot prints. After taking ten photos, she looked up at Amanda. "Okay, that should do it," she said and took her gun back. "Let's get inside."

Amanda gratefully turned and hurried back toward the kitchen. Once inside, she waited for Sarah and then slammed the kitchen door shut and locked it. "You are a crazy woman," she told Sarah, breathing hard.

"And you are a very brave friend," Sarah replied, and hugged her friend. "I'll never forget what you just did for me."

Amanda blushed a little and looked at the broom she was holding. "I'm not sure what I would have done if the intruder would have attacked us."

Sarah patted Amanda on her shoulder. "You would have knocked that person silly," she said. "Listen, hurry and get dressed okay? We have to drive into town."

"But, the snowballs...someone is out there," Amanda said, confused.

"Whoever is out there is trying to scare us into staying inside. We're going to do the opposite," Sarah answered in a calm voice. "Listen, June Bug, the weather outside is working for us and against us. The weather is also working for and against whoever is outside. And whoever is outside isn't going to be staying out there very long unless he or she wants hypothermia."

"This doesn't make any sense to me," Amanda confessed. "Why would someone brave this cold only to throw snowballs at your back door?"

"In my book," Sarah explained, putting her gun into the purse sitting next to the coffee pot, "the killer teased his victims. Sometimes he would throw snowballs at the victim's home as a way of letting them know he was watching them."

"Lovely," Amanda said in a horrified voice. "I'll...go get dressed now."

Sarah watched Amanda walk out of the kitchen and then hurried to the small pantry, yanked open the pantry door, studied the wooden shelves, and grabbed a green thermos. Then she ran back to the coffee pot, filled the thermos with coffee, closed it, set it down on the kitchen counter, and rushed to the back door. Easing the door open, she studied the crushed snowballs again and then focused on the snowy backyard. The winds were quickly erasing the boot tracks.

"Whoever you are..." she whispered in a shaky voice, "I'm not going to let you win."

Sarah closed the back door and glanced toward her purse. The sudden urge to grab her purse and make a run for it flushed through her veins. In all of her years working as a homicide detective, she had never had a killer stalk her. Sarah felt weak, helpless, wounded and trapped. The feeling was overwhelming and suffocating. "No," she scolded herself, "I will not run scared. I'm a cop...was a cop...still am a cop...by instinct..."

Sarah walked to the kitchen counter, snatched up her purse and the green thermos and walked into the living room. She set them down on the coffee table, calmly retrieved her coat from the coat rack and put it on, and then dug out a pair of warm brown gloves from the right coat pocket. "Stay at the ready," Sarah whispered to herself and slid the gloves onto her hands.

"I'm ready, in record time," Amanda announced, nearly running into the living room.

Sarah nodded and bent down. "Okay," she responded, checking the gun sitting in her ankle holster.

Amanda quickly tossed on her warm pink ski cap and then zipped up her thick coat. "Maybe you should take that gun out of your purse?" she asked. Not wasting any time, she pulled a set of pink gloves from her coat pocket and put them on.

"I have my backup. I want the stalker to think we're running scared. If I go charging toward my Subaru with a gun in my hand, the stalker..." Sarah paused.

"What?" Amanda asked in alarm.

"I said… 'stalker'… my goodness," Sarah whispered in a shaky voice. Turning from Amanda, she looked at the cold fireplace. "The Snowman Killer from Frostworth…he stalked, tormented…tortured…and then attacked…"

Amanda wasn't sure what to say or do. Now she was both terrified and confused. "Hey," she said, "Los Angeles, snap out of it, girl. We're making a run for town, remember?"

"Huh?" Sarah asked in a dazed voice as her mind recreated the image of the hideous snowman wearing the leather jacket. In her mind's eye, the snowman grinned at Sarah and began chewing on a peppermint candy cane. *"The weather outside is frightening…but the fire inside is deadly, Sarah…oh so deadly…"*

"Hey, Sarah!" Amanda yelled. She ran over to her friend and, with scared hands, began shaking her. "Snap out of it…snap out of it!"

"Huh?" Sarah repeated, still confused. Slowly, she looked into Amanda's worried eyes. "He attacks when the snow falls…"

"Who?" Amanda begged.

"The Snowman Killer from Frostworth," Sarah whispered.

Unable to take the suspense any longer, Amanda pulled back her right hand and slapped Sarah across the face with her glove. "Snap out of it!"

Shocked that her friend had slapped her, Sarah brought a hand to her face. "You…hit me…"

"Yes, I did," Amanda confessed. She hugged Sarah as tight as she could. "I know you're scared… I'm so scared I could turn into a block of ice…but we have to get into town."

Being slapped across the face had brought Sarah's mind back into focus. "I'm okay...thanks," she told Amanda, hugging her friend back. "You have one mean wallop, though."

"Thank me later. Right now, let's get into town," Amanda begged.

Sarah nodded. "Okay, we have to look like we're running scared. I'm not sure where the stalker...I mean...where our enemy is hiding outside, so we'll have no time to dilly-dally. Once I open the front door, run and don't stop running until you reach my Subaru."

"You can count on it," Amanda promised.

Sarah pointed at the coffee table. "Grab the thermos and my purse. I might need my hands free."

Amanda watched Sarah snatch the Subaru keys from the candy dish. She quickly grabbed the thermos and Sarah's purse. "I'm ready," she said in a nervous voice.

Without hesitating, Sarah unlocked the front door. "Here we go," she said and yanked the front door open. "Go!"

Chapter Eight

Amanda drew in a deep breath and raced past
Sarah. Sarah hurried outside, slammed the front
door, locked it, and ran toward her Subaru.
Unable to help herself, she looked toward the snowman. The
snowman appeared naked and angry. She could almost hear
it hissing at her, glaring with narrow, vicious eyes. "I will not
be afraid of you," Sarah whispered as she ran through the
knee-deep snow toward her car.

Meanwhile, Amanda made it to the car, looked over her
shoulder at Sarah, saw her friend looking at the creepy
snowman, and yelled, "Hurry!"

Sarah made her way around to the driver's side door and
pulled it open. Crawling into the driver's seat, she prayed the
Subaru's all-wheel-drive would be powerful enough to drive
on roads that had not been plowed yet. "Buckle up," she told
Amanda.

Amanda slammed the passenger's door shut and buckled

up. "Oh, the windshield is covered in snow. The windshield wipers won't be able to clear that much snow."

Sarah brought the Subaru to life. "Sit tight," she told Amanda and jumped back out into the snow. Using her hands, she began knocking snow off the windshield. As she worked to clear the snow, a snowball zoomed past her head and smacked into the windshield. Sarah became as still as a frozen chunk of ice. Even though she knew a human hand had thrown the snowball, the fear eating her alive was insisting that the hideous snowman had come to life and thrown the snowball at her. Before she could force her body to move, a second snowball struck, this time hitting her in the back. Out of instinct or perhaps sheer panic, Sarah broke through her paralysis, bent down, snatched the gun out of the ankle holster, turned, and unloaded a full clip in the direction of the snowman. When the clip was empty, she ran to the driver's side door and jumped into the seat.

"Get us out of here," Amanda begged.

Sarah threw the Subaru into reverse and pressed the gas pedal. The car struggled to move backward. The tires began to kick snow into the air in furious fits. "Come on...come on..." Sarah begged, pressing on the gas pedal.

"The snow is too high," Amanda said in a defeated voice.

Sarah didn't give up. She threw the Subaru into first gear and drove forward as much as the snow allowed, then backed up at full speed. She performed this routine numerous times until, at last, the Subaru was able to climb backwards, over the snow. "Here we go," Sarah told Amanda, sliding to a stop in the road and throwing the car into first gear again.

Amanda held her breath. Surely, she thought, the Subaru

would become stuck. But when it lunged forward, she yelled and clapped her hands in victory. "You did it!"

Sarah flicked on the windshield wipers. The windshield still had a good amount of snow on it, but the wipers began throwing it off. "To town we go," she told Amanda in a voice that sounded as if she was choking back vomit.

"Are you okay?" Amanda asked.

Sarah's voice came in tense bursts. "For a minute...I thought...the snowman had come alive...somehow..."

Amanda reached over and rubbed Sarah's shoulder. She didn't speak until Sarah pulled up in front of the coffee shop. Conrad was sitting in his truck, waiting. "I suggest we sleep in town tonight," Amanda said as she unbuckled her seat belt.

"I couldn't agree more," Sarah agreed.

She opened the driver's side door and got out of the car. A powerful gust of icy wind caused her to close her eyes, and she saw the hideous snowman again. "You're just snow...nothing more," she told it. "It's the flesh that's real."

Amanda walked around the Subaru to Sarah. "Here's your purse."

"Thanks," Sarah said. "Some morning, huh?"

"The day is still young," Amanda replied and nodded at Conrad, who was getting out of his truck.

"Let's get into the coffee shop."

Amanda looked at Conrad. The man wasn't wearing the black ski mask he had been wearing the night before. Instead, he had seemingly matured into a sensible black winter hat with ear guards that complemented his black coat. "Good morning," she called out and pointed at the front door of the coffee shop.

Conrad nodded and walked to the front door, pushing his legs through the knee-deep snow covering the sidewalk. Once inside, he waited until Sarah turned on the lights and then walked to the same table he had been sitting at the day before and grabbed a chair. "Coffee?" Sarah asked, taking off her coat.

Amanda shook the green thermos in her hands at Conrad. "Best coffee in the world," she promised.

"Sure," Conrad said and watched Sarah examine the back of her coat. By the way Sarah's brows were scrunched together in a frown, he could tell something had gone down at her cabin. He waited until Sarah brought three cups to the table before speaking. "Anything you want to tell me?" he asked, watching her open the thermos.

"We had a visitor this morning," Amanda confessed, sitting down across from Conrad, leaving Sarah to sit down beside him. She took off her coat and looked at Sarah. "Sarah was great, though. A real mama bear."

Sarah handed Amanda her cup of coffee and then handed a second cup to Conrad. As she sat down, she grabbed her own cup of coffee and looked toward the front door. "The stalker was at my cabin," she told Conrad. There was a pause.

Conrad looked at Amanda. Amanda slowly nodded. "Threw snowballs with rocks hidden in them at the back door and then threw a snowball at the Subaru as we were making our daring escape."

"A snowball hit me in the back. I unloaded a full clip in the direction it came from," Sarah added in a distant voice. "I'm not sure if I hit my target... I doubt it."

"Can I show the detective the photos you took of the boot prints?" Amanda asked.

Sarah nodded. Amanda put down her coffee, opened Sarah's purse, dug out the cell phone, brought up the photos of the boot prints, and handed the cell phone to Conrad. Conrad studied the photos. "Small feet," he said.

Sarah closed her eyes. "I know," she said in a miserable voice.

"Small feet...what does that mean? Oh, the tracks were made by a woman, is that it?" Amanda asked.

"Could be a man...but most likely a woman," Conrad answered as he methodically studied the photos Sarah had taken. He stopped when he accidentally scrolled too far and came upon a photo of Sarah dressed in a white wedding gown, hugging her ex-husband. Embarrassed, he handed the phone back to her. "Sarah, what do you think?"

Forcing her mind to reload, Sarah focused on Conrad. "The way the snowman was built...the height...the stalker is between 5'5" and 5'8". The boot prints are between a women's size 7 and 8. The stalker doesn't weigh very much because the boot prints—"

"Aren't as heavy as a man's would be," Conrad finished for her.

"So this slime ball is a woman," Amanda said.

"Most likely, but it's always wise to assume this person could be a man, too," Conrad replied.

"The stalker is probably a woman, though," Sarah confirmed. "The snowball she threw hit me in the back, but the power in the throw wasn't very strong."

Conrad sipped his coffee. "Who are you thinking it could be?"

"Tori Lucas...maybe? After all, we did end on a bad note back in Los Angeles," Sarah confessed. "There's one way to find out."

"Make the call," Conrad said.

Sarah stood up. "I'll be in the office."

"Want me to come with you?" Amanda asked.

"No," Sarah smiled at Amanda, "you stay here with Detective Spencer."

Chapter Nine

Sarah made her way into the kitchen. "Lucas...Tori Lucas, are you behind this?" she whispered. She opened the door to the cramped office and sat down at the desk. Pulling off her gloves, she tossed them down and began tapping the desk with her right pointer finger. "Tori Lucas..." she repeated and looked at the office phone sitting on the desk. "Okay, let's call some old friends."

Sarah picked up the phone and called someone who she knew was still working as a homicide detective in Los Angeles. Peter Greenfield picked up on the third ring. "Hello, stranger," he said in a gruff voice. Sitting far away in his stuffy office in Los Angeles with a cigar in his mouth, Peter tossed down a brown folder and put his cell phone on speakerphone. "To what do I owe the honor?"

"Hey Pete," Sarah said in a relieved voice, "I'm glad you took my call. I know I haven't called—"

"I should hang up and mail my boot to your backside," Peter griped. He puffed on his cigar. At the age of sixty-two, the man wasn't in any mood to show manners toward a friend who had essentially tossed cold water in his face.

"I know, I know..." Sarah admitted in a guilty voice. "What can I say, Pete? The divorce took the wind out of my sails. You can hate me and hang up now."

Peter looked down at his cell phone. Compassion broke his heart. He took the cigar out of his mouth and set it down in a metal ashtray, rubbed his thick gray beard, and then shook his head. "You know I can't turn my back on you, Cat."

Sarah chuckled. "No one has called me by that name in a long time. I have a close friend now who calls me 'Los Angeles,'" Sarah told Peter and nearly started to cry. "Listen, Pete," she said, fighting back her tears, "I need a favor. Can you see if Sergeant Tori Lucas is still on the force?"

Peter picked up his cell phone, swiveled around in his black office chair and looked out of the dusty window at a view of the mysterious city people in southern California called home. "Sergeant Lucas is still playing errand girl for the ties and suits around here. I saw her fetching coffee this morning."

Sarah didn't know whether to be relieved or upset. "Are you sure? What am I asking...of course you're sure."

"What's going on, Cat?" Peter asked, alarmed. "Why the sudden interest in that nosy goat?"

"Nothing I can't handle, Pete," Sarah promised. "It's sure great hearing your voice. How is Beth?"

"Fussy," Peter replied and rolled his eyes. "That woman finds more to fuss about in one minute than I can in an entire lifetime. Thank goodness for overtime."

Sarah smiled. Hearing Peter's voice was great. Old

memories began strolling into her worried mind. "You sure taught me a lot, you old grouch."

"And you sure were green behind the ears," Peter retorted. "Now cut the act and tell me what's going on up there with the polar bears. I heard some hotshot from New York moved into your neck of the woods, and now you're talking about Lucas. Spill the beans, Cat."

"I wish I could, Pete, I really do...but the truth is, I don't know what's going on. I thought maybe Lucas might have had a vendetta against me."

"Because you chewed her down to size?" Peter asked.

"I was in a very bad mood that day, Pete. I shouldn't have been so hard on the woman."

"Yeah, you should have. Everyone in this department is sick and tired of Lucas sneaking around with her hungry eyes."

"The important thing is that I was wrong," Sarah said.

"Wrong about what?" Peter demanded.

"I'm not sure yet," Sarah confessed. She wanted to tell Peter about being Milly Stevens, about the "The Snowman Killer from Frostworth" series she was writing, about the hideous snowman...the rock snowballs...everything...but she couldn't. "Do me a favor, will you?"

"If I can, Cat. I'm in the middle of a case right now. A John Doe was found washed up on the beach yesterday."

"See if anyone I sent off to prison has been paroled recently, will you? If anyone we know has been set free, give me a call, okay?" Sarah tried to control her voice, but it wavered with fear.

"Sure, sure," Peter said, hearing the desperation in his old partner's voice. "I'll give you a call back in a few hours."

"Call my cell phone." Sarah gave him her cell phone number. "If you can't get through, try the number I'm calling you on now."

"Cat," Peter said in a stern voice, "if you're in trouble and you're not telling me, so help me, I'll drive up to that frozen tundra you're calling home and put my foot up your backside."

"Thanks, Pete," Sarah said in a grateful voice. "Call me, okay?"

"Sure, sure," Peter sighed. "Give me a few hours."

"You're the best, Pete. Bye." Sarah hung up the phone and wiped tears away from her eyes. "I miss you, Pete," she whispered.

Sarah returned to the front room. "Sergeant Lucas is currently in Los Angeles," she informed Conrad and sat down.

Conrad rubbed his chin. "Okay, but that still doesn't take away that the person in question is a woman."

"I know," Sarah said. She focused on Amanda. "I'm starving. What about you?"

"Famished," Amanda said. Hearing a snow plow go by outside, she smiled. "The diner should be open."

"Sounds good to me."

"Wait a minute," Conrad interjected. "Last night I found out the leather jacket wrapped around that snowman sitting on your front lawn came from the department store here in town. I have Andrew at the store right now."

"Doing what?" Amanda asked.

"Back-checking the purchase," Sarah explained. "Andrew will check to see how many leather jackets were sold, when, and by what means—cash, check or credit card."

"Maybe we can track down a specific time and catch the person who bought the leather jacket on camera. I heard this Old Man O'Mally is very paranoid about theft," Conrad said. He finished off his coffee. It was way too strong, but he didn't mind.

"Paranoid, but cheap," Amanda pointed out in a frustrated voice. "O'Mally's store has dummy cameras set up everywhere. As far as checks or credit cards, forget it. He makes everyone pay with cash only. And every purchase in his store is rung up on an old-fashioned, dinosaur cash register."

"Oh dear, I totally forgot about that," Sarah agreed. "About the only thing Andrew is going to track down is a dead end. And he knows that, so why would he go in the first place?" Sarah wondered. Then another thought struck her. "Unless...he knows something we don't. Amanda, we'll grab a candy bar at O'Mally's. Come on."

"Wait a minute," Conrad told Sarah. "Calm down. Let Andrew do his job. He'll report his findings to me and I'll share them with you."

"No, thanks," Sarah said and stood up. "Detective Spencer...once a cop, always a cop. I have work to do. You're either with me or sitting on the sidelines."

"You go, girl," Amanda said proudly and jumped to her feet.

Conrad slowly stood up as well and locked eyes with Sarah. "We work as a team from this point forward. Are we clear?"

"A team," Sarah agreed. "But Amanda is part of our team. Is that clear?"

Conrad looked at Amanda. The British woman put her arm around Sarah's shoulder. "We come as a duo, take it or leave it."

"Don't shoot yourself in the foot," Conrad told Amanda and walked outside.

"Don't shoot yourself in the foot," Amanda fussed, imitating Conrad's voice, and made a snarly face at his retreating back. "Pip, pip, cheerio."

"Grab your coat and come on," Sarah said. "We've got work to do, partner."

Back at Sarah's cabin, two cold hands worked to build a second snowman. "One snowman to go, Sarah...and then the snow will stop falling for you...for good..." the voice whispered. Then it began to sing. Ten minutes later, a snowman appeared wearing a leather jacket and chewing on a peppermint candy cane.

Chapter Ten

As he stood in the toy aisle, Andrew was surprised to see Conrad walking toward him. He quickly put down the toy baby he'd been holding. "Hello, Detective... I was..."

"Looking for a toy for your two-year-old niece who has a birthday coming up next week," Amanda winked at Andrew.

Andrew held out his wrists. "Guilty as charged."

"Find out anything?" Conrad asked. He felt uneasy standing in an aisle lined with baby dolls staring at him with creepy, lifelike eyes. He could never understand why parents bought their young ones creepy baby dolls.

Sarah studied Andrew's kind face. Grateful to be in a warm department store surrounded by friends, she felt prepared to tackle this case bravely with both hands. "Detective Spencer and I are working together."

Andrew looked at Conrad. Conrad nodded. "Okay," Andrew said and rubbed the back of his neck from exhaustion. "I talked with Old Man O'Mally about twenty minutes ago. He said unless I had a warrant, he wasn't going to give one single crumb of information. Sorry, I hit a brick wall, guys."

"Where is he now?" Conrad demanded in a tough voice.

"Now calm down, Detective," Andrew said and held his hands up in the air. "Old Man O'Mally has every right to be tight-lipped. And unless we go get a warrant from Judge McKay, all we can do in his store is shop or leave."

Sarah looked up at the ceiling, which was lined with rows and rows of fluorescent light bulbs. The light falling down from the ceiling felt cold even though warm air was blasting from overhead air vents. "Amanda, let's take a walk and go have a look at the leather jackets."

Andrew rubbed the back of his neck again. "Listen, guys, I've only had a couple of hours of sleep. I think I'll head back to the station and grab a nap in one of the cells. My mind feels like slush right now."

"Yeah, go ahead," Conrad said, sounding irritated, "but before you do, call Judge McKay and get that warrant. I want Old Man O'Mally singing like a canary."

Andrew nodded and walked away.

"Let's go," Sarah told Amanda.

Together, Sarah and Amanda walked toward the back right-hand side of the store where Old Man O'Mally had placed the women's clothing department. The store was empty of customers, which Sarah appreciated. "Why do you want to see the leather jackets?" Amanda asked.

"Maybe some glitter," Sarah answered, spotting a wooden clothing rack lined with black leather jackets. "It's almost like being back in Los Angeles," she told Amanda in a nostalgia voice. "The stores...the people...the traffic...the smells...the sounds..."

Amanda looked around. All her eyes saw were clothing racks lined with overpriced women's clothes that were mostly tacky. "If you say so, Los Angeles, but what does glitter have to do with all of this chaos?"

Sarah approached the leather jackets and stopped. Looking around the clothing section, she spotted a rack of cheesy nightgowns with goofy cartoon figures on them. "The rock snowballs had glitter in them," she explained.

Amanda casually touched a leather jacket. "You must have eyes like a hawk."

"Actually, I wear reading glasses," Sarah confessed humorously. She turned her full attention to the leather jackets. With focused eyes and skilled hands, she checked each jacket carefully. Amanda stepped back and watched. "I didn't see buckets of glitter...just little pieces," Sarah explained. "When we arrived in town, I noticed a few pieces of glitter on the windshield of my Subaru. I also noticed some glitter on the back of my coat."

"What does that mean?" Amanda asked.

Sarah stopped at a certain leather jacket. Narrowing her eyes, she focused on the inside tag. With her right pointer finger, she gently pushed the tag upward. "Bingo," she said. "Look at this, June Bug."

Amanda hurried over to Sarah. Excitement filled her heart instead of fear. It felt incredible to actually be tracking down clues instead of running scared. "By golly, I believe you've found something," she said, spotting a few pieces of glitter on the tag.

Sarah grabbed the wooden hanger the leather jacket was hanging on. "Let's find—"

"Mr. Incognito," Amanda sighed and tossed a thumb at the rack of cheesy gowns. Conrad was standing next to the gowns watching Sarah.

Sarah looked over at Conrad and motioned for him to walk over to her. "What did you find?" he asked.

"Glitter," Sarah explained and pointed at the glitter on the tag.

"Sarah saw glitter in the snowballs thrown at the back door, on the windshield of her Subaru, and on the back of her coat," Amanda explained, hoping to sound all cop-like.

"I need to see the leather jacket you took off the snowman," Sarah told Conrad in an urgent voice and handed him the jacket she was holding.

"The jacket is in my office back at the police station," Conrad replied, studying the small traces of glitter on the tag of the leather jacket. "We might be able to pull matching prints. Good work, Detective."

"No," Sarah said, dodging the compliment, "the stalker made a mistake, that's all. If...it was a mistake, that is?"

"What do you mean?" Conrad asked.

Before responding, Sarah paused and allowed the warm environment of the department store to soothe her. She enjoyed the feeling of department stores and was especially fond of old department stores. Of course, she liked to shop, but it was the joy of being in a comforting place that mattered. Even though O'Mally's was only a medium-sized store sitting on the edge of a small Alaskan town, Sarah found it to be friendly and welcoming.

Finally, she took a deep breath and answered Conrad's question. "In the series I'm writing, the killer leaves false clues to confuse his victim and make the police chase their own tails."

Amanda nearly slapped her own head. "And you think—"

"It's possible...but then again, I'm not so sure," Sarah interrupted. "We need to run prints off this jacket and the jacket in your office, Detective Spencer, and see what develops."

Conrad began to reply when he spotted a young, chubby, black-haired girl watching him from behind a rack of sweaters. "Young lady?" he called out.

The girl stiffened and looked around. She was wearing a light green work vest with a name tag attached to it. Thinking fast, she tried to pretend to be an employee working in the clothing department. "I was just wondering if you needed any help?" she asked Conrad in a friendly but nervous voice.

Amanda recognized the girl first. "Rhonda Nettles, you were eavesdropping," she scolded.

"No...honest... I..." Rhonda struggled to defend herself. Then, unable to continue, she threw her eyes down at her shoes. "Okay...you caught me. I was eavesdropping."

"Why?" Sarah asked.

Rhonda tried to look up at Sarah. Sarah was so beautiful and she was so chubby and drab—just a chubby teenager working a dead-end job. "I work as a cashier and a stock girl here," she whispered. "If Mr. O'Mally catches me, he'll fire me."

"It's okay," Sarah assured her. "Mr. O'Mally is nowhere in sight."

Rhonda looked into Sarah's strong eyes, unaware of the pain the woman was holding inside of her heart. "I put the jackets out myself," she whispered. "I helped unload the biweekly shipment when it arrived four days ago."

Conrad rubbed his chin. Something in Rhonda's voice made him take notice. "How many leather jackets were there total?" he asked.

"Four large, four medium, and four small," Rhonda answered, not daring to look Conrad in his eyes. "Mr. O'Mally ordered them because the new store in Fairbanks is selling them, but as you can see, the jackets aren't really moving. I only sold three so far."

"Three?" Sarah gasped. Spinning herself around, she began digging through the leather jackets. "Four large...here are the four mediums...and...and...the smalls are all missing except for the one we have." Turning around, she focused on Rhonda. With her heart racing wildly, she forced herself to take a deep breath and attempted to calm down. "You sold the jackets?"

"Yes, ma'am," Rhonda answered in a meek voice.

"To who?" Sarah asked very carefully. "Can you describe what the person looked like?"

"Some girl, maybe my age or a little older. I never saw her before in my life. But what I did notice was how much glitter nail polish she was wearing," Rhonda answered.

Amanda began to speak, but Sarah quickly shook her head at her. "Go on," she urged Rhonda.

"Well," Rhonda said, looking around for Mr. O'Mally,

"she was wearing a pink winter cap...a pink coat...white ski pants...and black boots. She was very pretty. I admired how stylish she looked. And...oh yeah...she had a red ponytail."

"Anything else?" Conrad asked in a gentle tone.

"Well," Rhonda said, thinking, "oh, she had a funny accent. It was obvious she wasn't from here. She talked...kinda like you," Rhonda finished and pointed at Conrad.

Conrad glanced up at the dummy cameras attached to certain areas of the ceiling. "Being cheap doesn't pay," he said in a frustrated voice.

"Did this girl say anything to you?" Sarah asked Rhonda.

"Oh, sure," Rhonda said. "We talked while I rang up her purchase...chit-chat talk, mostly. She seemed super friendly. She even complimented my new nose ring...but I think it's kinda dorky. But this guy I like thinks nose rings are cool, you know."

Sarah stepped forward and put a hand on Rhonda's shoulder. "What else did you two talk about? Please, it's very important."

Rhonda looked at Sarah, then at Amanda, and finally at Conrad. "Ms. Garland, I only work here part-time. My family isn't exactly rich. I need the money I earn here. I don't want to get in trouble with O'Mally."

Sarah took her hand off Rhonda's shoulder. She opened her pocketbook and pulled out her purse. "Here," she said, popping open her green wallet and pulling out a wad of twenty dollar bills, "this is five hundred dollars. I'm hiring you to talk to me for a few minutes."

Rhonda stared at the money. "I...yeah, hey, sure," she said, suddenly beaming like a ray of sunshine.

"What did the girl say to you?"

"Let me think...we talked about the weather...nail polish because I complimented her fingernails...clothes...boys, of course...and that was about it," Rhonda told Sarah.

"Did she buy anything other than the jackets?" Sarah asked in a strained voice.

"Just one of those creepy mystery books...the one written by some lady named Milly Stevens. My mother loves her work," Rhonda explained. "And...oh yeah, she bought a small crowbar? Strange."

"Was anyone with her?" Sarah asked, glancing at Conrad. Conrad nodded.

"No, ma'am."

"By chance, did you see what she was driving?" Sarah asked.

"Well..." Rhonda said, looking down at her feet again, "I did kinda look out into the parking lot when she left. I thought for sure a girl like her might be driving a BMW or Porsche, you know. But...well, she didn't get into any kind of car. She just kinda walked away and headed back toward town. It was snowing pretty good, too. I remember thinking she was going to freeze."

Sarah pushed the wad of twenty dollar bills into Rhonda's hand. "Thanks, Rhonda. You've been a great help. Now do me a favor, ditch the nose ring and be yourself. The right guy will come along and love you for who you are, not what you look like."

"You sound like my mother," Rhonda sighed. "I'd better get back up front."

Conrad waited until Rhonda walked away before speaking. "Detective Garland, what're your thoughts?" he asked.

"A very deranged fan," Sarah replied. "Let's run the jackets and see what we come up with. Maybe we'll match prints?"

"You had no doubt that the suspect would be a woman all along," Conrad pointed out.

Sarah shrugged her shoulders. "The damage to the window sill in my writing room seemed to have been made by someone who wasn't familiar with a crowbar. From the damage, it was clear the person who broke into my home was an amateur."

"Maybe an amateur with a crowbar," Conrad mentioned. "She could be very skilled with a weapon."

Amanda couldn't believe some mentally abnormal teenage girl had scared the wits out of her. And why were Sarah and Conrad talking as if they were still concerned? "All of this fright over a silly teenage girl?" she asked and then rolled her eyes. "Blimey, I thought the person was a killer bear. Sarah and I were running for our lives this morning...and from what? A silly twit! Blimey."

"Never underestimate a killer," Sarah warned Amanda. "Sometimes the people who you think are the least of threats turn out to be the deadliest of all. This girl is still a threat, and I will treat her as one."

"A silly teenage twit?" Amanda asked, rolling her eyes again.

"A silly teenage girl in Minnesota now sits in prison," Conrad told Amanda. "People call her the 'Closet Killer'."

Sarah held up five fingers. "Five boyfriends dead. Five boys who thought they were dating a silly twit. Never underestimate a killer," she emphasized.

Amanda swallowed. "Five?"

"Five," Sarah said and walked away. "You coming, partner?"

"Uh...sure," Amanda said and hurried after Sarah.

Conrad drew in a deep breath and followed behind Amanda. "Shouldn't be too hard tracking down a silly twit," he whispered in a worried voice.

Outside, the snow continued to fall. Back at Sarah's cabin, two hideous snowmen stood on the front lawn, chewing peppermint candy canes, staring at the window attached to Sarah's writing room. Behind the cabin, a shadowy figure walked back to a pair of skis and began singing to herself. "Oh, the weather outside is frightful...but the fire is so delightful...and since we've no place to go, let it snow, let it snow, let it snow."

Chapter Eleven

Sarah pulled back the cobalt blue curtain covering the window in Conrad's office. Night was falling. "The storm is getting worse," she said, staring at heavily falling snow being thrown in every direction imaginable by angry, icy winds.

Conrad sat at his desk with his right leg tossed over the corner edge. He picked up a black pen and began tapping it on his right knee cap. "I never thought I would see the day," he replied.

Sarah folded her arms together. "We extracted good prints from the jackets, even if we were forced to use the old-fashioned method."

"At least this station has a fax machine," Conrad said in a frustrated voice. "Now all we can do is sit tight and wait while the prints are being examined."

Sarah continued to stare out into the snow. Her mind was struggling to make sense of the case. Hearing her cell phone ring from inside of her purse, she let go of the curtains and walked over to Conrad's desk. "This call might be important," she told Conrad and fished out her phone. "It's Peter," she said in a grateful voice and answered the call. "Hey Pete, what's the news?"

Peter sat in his old car outside of a closed-down seaside hotdog stand, looking out at calm waves brushing up against an empty beach. "I did some checking, Cat. Your list of foes are all still securely behind bars, except for a woman named Veronica Wilson."

"Veronica Wilson...doesn't ring a bell," Sarah said. She sat down in the cushioned gray chair in front of Conrad's desk.

"I didn't think it would. You arrested Veronica Wilson when you were a rookie cop, fresh out of the Academy," Peter answered. Looking down into the passenger's seat, he studied a warm box of pizza. "Veronica Wilson was arrested for attempted murder."

"Pete, we're talking years ago," Sarah said, desperately trying to think back. "Help me out here, okay?"

"She was sentenced to twenty years in prison, Cat. She was released six months ago. But..."

"But what?" Sarah pressed as the icy winds outside the police station smashed into the office window with furious fists.

Peter grabbed a slice of cheese pizza and took a bite. "The woman turned up dead on the same beach I'm looking at now. The death was ruled a suicide."

Sarah sat silently for a minute as her mind attempted to forge a connection between Veronica Wilson and the case in Alaska. "Did she have a daughter?"

Conrad stopped tapping the pen against his knee and perked up his ears. "Put the call on speakerphone," he whispered.

Sarah nodded and hit the speakerphone button. "Pete, I have Detective Spencer with me. I have you on speakerphone now, is that okay?"

"Fine with me," Peter answered, chewing his pizza. His eyes drifted past the closed hotdog stand and focused on the deserted beach. "I'm wondering why a woman fresh out of prison would drown herself?"

"Did Veronica Wilson have a daughter, Pete?" Sarah asked again.

"Veronica birthed a baby girl before she was hauled away in handcuffs," Peter told Sarah. "Brad Wilson, the husband and intended victim, took full custody of the baby and moved away to New York."

Conrad grabbed a pen and pad of paper and began taking down notes. "What was the name of the baby?" Sarah asked.

"Kaley Wilson," Peter answered. "I ran a check on her." He paused and finished off his pizza. "Where's my cigar?"

"Pete, please," Sarah begged.

"Cigar first," Peter fussed. Leaning over, he snatched open the glove compartment and saw a half-smoked cigar. "Ah, there you are," he said and grabbed it. "Now, where were we?"

"You ran a check, Kaley Wilson," Sarah said and rolled her eyes. She had nearly forgotten how stubborn Peter could be unless he had a cigar in his mouth.

"Kaley Wilson," Peter said, now searching for a pack of matches, "is nineteen years old. She currently resides in Los

Angeles and works as a fashion model. Pretty young girl, but nothing special, you know. She models clothes for her old man, who owns makeup lines, nail polish lines, all that girly stuff, and a clothing line, too." Peter spotted a box of matches sitting on the dashboard and grabbed them. "The newest line Kaley's old man is pushing is stuff that deals with glitter...glittery clothes, makeup, nail polish, hair spray, the works....plain dumb to me."

Sarah looked at Conrad. "Pete, remind me to give you a big kiss someday," she said. "You're my hero."

"Hero?" Peter repeated, lighting his cigar. "Listen, Cat, you ditched me and ran off with the polar bears. It took me years to train you and form you into the detective you are today, and how do you thank me?"

"Pete, I—"

"Yeah, yeah, save it for the Eskimos," Peter complained and puffed on his cigar. "Listen, I think we have a homicide and not a suicide on our hands."

"It could be," Sarah agreed. "Where is Brad Wilson? Did he relocate back to Los Angeles with his daughter?"

"Nah, the guy is still in New York."

Sarah bit down on her lower lip. "Can you check and see if Kaley or Brad Wilson ever visited Veronica Wilson while she was in prison?"

"Already did," Peter said. "Kaley began visiting her mother in prison when she moved out to Los Angeles. Brad kept his distance."

"I see," Sarah said. "Did Veronica have any other visitors, other than her daughter?"

"Not a single one," Peter replied in a voice that almost

seemed sad. "I checked the woman's medical records. Veronica suffered from manic depression. Prison life made her condition worse. We're talking about fights, trips to solitary, attempted suicides, the works. Lady was on some serious medication, too."

"And you think whoever killed Veronica used her mental state to cover up the murder, right?"

"Bingo," Peter said and then grew silent. As he stared down at the beach, he knew something horrible had happened, and its horrible effects were still taking place.

Something in Peter's voice was bugging Sarah. "Pete, what are you hiding from me? You're telling me the ingredients to the cake, but you're leaving off the cherry. What is it?"

"Cat..." Peter began to speak and then grew silent again. Debating on whether to release the absolute truth to Sarah or not, he took a puff on his cigar. "Cat, Veronica Wilson blamed you for ruining her life. Your name was carved into the walls of her prison cell...nasty letters addressed to you were found... I'm sure you get the picture."

"I get the picture," Sarah sighed. "The picture is becoming all too clear. There are a few missing pieces, but I'm sure I'll kick them out from under my desk soon enough."

"So, what's going on on your end? I want straight answers, are we clear? If you try to fire blanks at me I'll hang up," Peter warned.

Sarah focused on Conrad's face. Her eyes told the detective that she felt she had to confess the truth to her old friend. Conrad bit down on his lower lip and hesitantly nodded. "Go ahead," his eyes told Sarah. She drew in a deep breath, eased her mind into a dark room and closed the door. "When you stand in darkness, Pete, there's always a scream waiting to capture you."

"I'm listening," Peter said.

"Yesterday I found a snowman in my yard...wearing a leather jacket." Sarah slowly explained what she had been experiencing to Peter, who listened with skilled ears. Sarah finished with the leather jackets. "Detective Spencer and I managed to pull some prints. We're waiting for the results."

Peter chewed on his cigar. "Okay, it appears that Kaley Wilson may be the skunk in the woods."

"Kaley Wilson may be seeking revenge for her mother," Sarah said. "It's possible she broke into my writing room without my knowing, looking for ways to get revenge, and that's how she came across my book."

Conrad considered Sarah's suggestion. Remaining quiet, he stood up and walked to the office window, pulled back the curtains, and looked out into the storm.

"She needed an edge on you," Peter replied, "and your book gave her the edge."

"I know," Sarah said miserably. "Kaley Wilson can kill me the way the Snowman Killer from Frostworth kills his victims, and then escape into the snow without anyone knowing. If it wasn't for the glitter..."

"The glitter," Peter agreed. "I'm faxing you a photo of Kaley Wilson. Take the photo to the store clerk tomorrow and get a certified match."

"You got it, Pete," Sarah promised. "And hey, thanks for all of your help. I can't put into words how much...I miss you."

"Don't try," Peter told Sarah in a soft voice. "Listen, Cat, let's focus on this case. The killer I'm after is possibly the same girl who's after you. I can't fly up to polar bear land, which leaves this case directly in your lap. You're flying solo – well, with Detective Spencer. The guy is a good cop, so trust him, okay?"

"How do you know that?" Sarah asked.

"I checked into Spencer. He has an impressive record including sustaining a few gunshot wounds. Guy has been shot four times, nearly died twice," Peter explained. "Listen, I'd better go. I need to take a walk on the beach. Call me when you get the results of the prints. I'll fax over Kaley Wilson's photo as soon as I get back to the station."

"I will...and thanks," Sarah said in a voice that clearly told Conrad how much she truly missed her old friend. "Bye, Pete."

"Bye, Cat."

Sarah put her cell phone away. Conrad had his back to her. "Shot four times?" she asked.

"Part of the job," Conrad responded in a humble voice. "Hey, where's Amanda with the coffee?"

Sarah studied Conrad. The man was a mystery to her. "I need to call Rhonda's home," she told him. "I can't wait until tomorrow to see if Kaley Wilson is the girl who bought the leather jackets."

"Okay," Conrad agreed. Turning away from the window, he looked into Sarah's beautiful face. He saw pain, hurt and sadness tearing the woman's heart apart. "I'll go see where Amanda and—"

Before Conrad could finish his sentence Andrew burst

into the office. "Bad news, Detective," he said, breathing hard, "Rhonda Nettles was attacked outside of O'Mally's while walking to her truck tonight."

Amanda pushed past Andrew. "We need to get to the hospital," she told Sarah.

"Let's go," Sarah said and snatched her coat off the metal coat rack standing in the corner of the office.

Chapter Twelve

Forty-five minutes later, after painfully driving less than fifteen miles per hour through a storm that was close to transforming into a raging blizzard, Sarah reached the hospital with Amanda. She parked in a snow-covered parking lot designated as 'Guest Parking' and waited until Conrad pulled in beside her in his truck. "Now why would Kaley attack Rhonda...if it was Kaley, that is?" Sarah asked Amanda.

"I don't know," Amanda answered, staring through the windshield into the snowstorm. "If a plow doesn't run by soon, we're not going to be able to drive back to the police station," she observed.

Sarah agreed. "Come on, let's get into the hospital," she said in a worried voice.

Getting out of her car, Sarah looked toward the hospital. It was a simple one-story brick building that had once been home to an elementary school. Snow-covered woods stood to the north, east and west side of the hospital. Only the south side had been cleared for parking, patient pick-up and drop-off, ambulances and delivery trucks. Sarah felt the darkness of the woods leering at her. *The snow, Sarah... when the snow stops falling...when the snow stops falling...*

"Let's hurry," Amanda said, making her way to Sarah and taking her hand.

Sarah saw Conrad get out of his truck. Andrew didn't follow. "Where is Andrew?" she called out over the wind.

"I sent him to O'Mally's," Conrad yelled, blocking the snow from his face with his right hand. "Let's get inside."

Feeling like a dark shadow had suddenly wrapped its hideous claws around her snowy little town, Sarah shivered and hurried toward the front entrance. She stepped through the sliding glass door into a modest lobby covered with white tile then immediately turned around and looked outside, suddenly expecting to see a snowman wearing a leather jacket and chewing a peppermint candy cane. "What is it?" Amanda asked, shaking the snow off her coat.

"Nothing," Sarah said and brushed the snow off her own coat.

Conrad examined the lobby. The room was medium-sized. The north wall was lined with brown leather sitting chairs separated by two coffee tables holding old magazines. An information desk stood against the east wall. A set of wooden double doors rested on the west wall. Beyond the double doors stood a hallway that twisted into the hospital. "No welcome party," Conrad said and pointed to the empty information desk.

"I'm sure we won't need a map," Amanda told Conrad and walked toward the set of double doors.

"It doesn't make sense that no one's at the info desk," Sarah said to Conrad as they followed behind Amanda.

"I know," Conrad agreed. "It could—" He stopped mid-sentence as the cell phone in his coat pocket rang. He pulled the phone out and checked the incoming caller. "Andrew," he told Sarah and answered the call. "Yes, Andrew...a witness? Mr. O'Mally himself? Sure, I'll get back to the station and talk to him as soon as possible. Please tell Mr. O'Mally we appreciate his cooperation."

Sarah watched Conrad put away his cell phone and began to ask a question when a *thud* struck the sliding glass doors behind them. Spinning around, Sarah saw the remains of a snowball sliding down the glass. With her heart racing, she watched as a second snowball struck the doors. Conrad pulled out his gun. "We have a visitor," he said in a calm voice.

Sarah opened her purse and followed suit, pulling out her own gun. "Amanda, go to Rhonda and stay there," she ordered.

Amanda didn't argue. She hurried through the double doors and vanished. "Easy now," Conrad said and cautiously eased toward the sliding glass doors as a third snowball smashed against the glass.

"Wait," Sarah said and grabbed Conrad's arm.

"What?"

Sarah bit down on her lower lip. "Kaley Wilson could have attacked Rhonda in order to draw us to the hospital, but that doesn't make sense. In my book, the killer attacks his victims at their residence. He never... I mean, Gary Hardcastle never draws his victims into public places. He stalks them in public places, but the victim never knows when he is watching."

"Gary Hardcastle, the name of your killer in the book?"

"Yes," Sarah said, staring at the sliding glass doors. "Something isn't right here, Conrad. Watch my back. I need to check out the snowballs."

"Okay."

Sarah eased toward the sliding glass doors, drew in a deep breath, put her gun at the ready, and stepped outside. Squinting into the snow and the wind, she struggled to spot Kaley Wilson, or anyone at all. Only seeing darkness, however, she shook her head, squatted down, scooped up the remains of a splattered snowball and walked back inside. "Hold my gun," she told Conrad.

Conrad took Sarah's gun and waited as she examined the snow in her hands. "Here's a rock...but...there's no glitter... They must not have thrown it very hard since it didn't break the glass," Sarah said in a puzzled voice as she examined the snow in her gloved hands with brilliant eyes.

Conrad leaned down and looked into Sarah's hands. He didn't spot any glitter, either. "We have a different attacker."

"Could be." Sarah brushed the snow off of her gloves and took her gun back from Conrad. "Detective, please stay in the lobby. I'm going to talk with Rhonda."

"Hurry," Conrad told her.

Sarah nodded, put her gun away, and ran off toward the double doors. Pushing them open, she entered a long, carpeted hallway littered with bad art. Ignoring the art, Sarah focused on her thoughts as she made her way toward the emergency room. A few minutes later, she stepped into a small, cramped room that smelled like alcohol and disinfectant. The room was home to a single bed, a heart monitor and a sitting chair. Amanda was standing next to the bed, looking down at Rhonda. "How is she?" Sarah asked.

"I'm okay," Rhonda said, sounding healthy but scared.

Sarah walked to the hospital bed and looked down. Rhonda looked up at her with a face that appeared to have no wounds. The girl was still wearing her work coat, and for all intents and purposes, she appeared fine. "I'm sorry, Rhonda, but Andrew made it seem like you were hurt more than what you appear to be?" Sarah asked.

Rhonda lifted her right hand and pointed to her back. "Someone ran up behind me and hit me in the back with something hard. I guess I might have been hurt except that I was wearing a lot of cushioning under my coat."

"Thank goodness," Sarah said.

"Not really," Amanda told Sarah, concerned. "Rhonda, tell Sarah what your attacker said."

Rhonda stared up at Sarah with frightened eyes. "The person who hit me was a guy...he warned me to never talk to you again or else he would kill me."

"Any idea who the person was?" Sarah asked.

"His voice was muffled, but I knew who it was," Rhonda said in a voice that suddenly became sad. Tears began falling from her eyes. "Sarah, why would Officer Edwin's son hurt me? We work together at O'Mally's. And why would he make his voice try to sound girlish?"

"Officer Edwin's son?" Sarah asked.

Rhonda nodded and wiped at her tears. "Philip was always kinda mean, but I never thought he would hurt me. And why would he care if he saw me talking to you?"

"I think I know," Sarah said and wiped Rhonda's tears away. "And I think I know why Mr. O'Mally is suddenly willing to perform his civic duty, too. Listen, you rest. Amanda is going to stay with you."

"My mother will be here soon. I'll be fine."

"Amanda will stay with you," Sarah repeated in a firm, loving voice. "You're a very brave young woman. When you get better, Amanda and I are going to take you out for a girl's night out dinner."

Amanda smiled. "Sure we will," she promised Rhonda.

"Stay with her," Sarah told Amanda and patted her friend's shoulder. "Hopefully before daybreak, this case will be solved."

Amanda watched Sarah walk away. "Hopefully when morning arrives you will still be alive," she whispered.

Chapter Thirteen

Sarah returned to the lobby and met Conrad, who was still standing guard near the information desk. "Call Andrew for me, please."

Conrad put his gun down on the desk, pulled out his cell phone, and made the call. "Here you go."

Sarah took the cell phone. "Andrew... Yes, it's Sarah... I need Officer Edwin's phone number... Please, no questions," Sarah said, studying the sliding doors. She saw a minor crack that had not been there before. "More snowballs?" she asked Conrad.

"Two more," Conrad confirmed.

"What?... No, I don't have a pen or piece of paper... Just tell me the number and I'll remember... Okay... Yes...thanks, Andrew." Sarah ended the call and dialed Officer Edwin's cell phone number. Officer Edwin picked up on the second ring. "Officer Edwin, this is Sarah Garland... No, everything is not fine, I'm afraid. Officer Edwin, Rhonda Nettles was attacked tonight... You heard?... I questioned Rhonda a few minutes ago and she said it was your son who attacked her. Where is your son?"

Conrad stared at Sarah. Obviously, the woman had a plan, but he wasn't sure what her plan was. Sarah nodded her eyes toward the sliding glass doors. "Get ready to go outside," she whispered to Conrad. "What's that, Officer Edwin?... Your son is at a friend's house studying? What friend? I see... Call and confirm. But before you do, can I ask if your son has a cell phone? He does...good. Then do me a favor, call your son's cell phone, repeatedly, until I call you and tell you to stop... Why?... Officer Edwin, I believe your son is involved in something very dangerous. Please, do as I ask and—"

Conrad took the cell phone away from Sarah. "Officer Edwin, this is Detective Spencer. We have a killer loose in town and your son might be helping this killer. Now do as we ask or hang up your badge... Good." Conrad shoved the cell phone back into his pocket. "We don't have time to be nice."

"Edwin is a decent man who is married to a sweet woman," Sarah snapped at Conrad. "You had no right to speak to him like that."

"Hate me later," Conrad told her. "We'd better get outside and listen to see if we can hear a cell phone start ringing. That is your plan, right?"

"Yes, it is," Sarah said. "Stay at the ready. This kid attacked Rhonda. He's proved he's dangerous."

"Why the snowballs?" Conrad asked as he picked up his gun.

Sarah looked Conrad deep in his eyes. "The kid outside isn't part of my book. He's playing out of character. I think I know why, too. Let's go."

"Stay alert," Conrad warned Sarah and followed her outside into the snow.

Sarah lowered her chin and walked toward the snowy tree line resting across the parking lot. "Philip," she yelled into the snow, hoping to be heard above the icy, howling winds, "we know it was you who attacked Rhonda. Stop throwing snowballs and come out and talk with us."

Conrad walked past Sarah with his gun aimed at the dark snow-covered trees. Lowering his eyes down to the snow, he spotted a set of boot prints. "I'm going to track this kid down."

Sarah examined the snowy trees. "Philip, let us help you. We know you're scared," she yelled. "I called your dad and informed him that you attacked Rhonda."

"You what?" a furious voice yelled from behind the trees. And then, faintly, the sound of a ringtone in the form of a country song drifted through the wind into Sarah's ears.

"That will be your father calling you," Sarah yelled to Philip.

"Boy," Conrad hollered in a loud, stern voice, "you have till the count of three to come out or I'm going to start shooting straight into the trees. I see your boot prints in the snow. If I don't take you out with my first clip, I'll reload and hunt you down."

"Let us help you," Sarah called out. Blocking snow from her eyes, she studied the trees. "Philip, did Kaley betray you? Is that what happened? She used you and then betrayed you? So you attacked Rhonda pretending to be Kaley, and now you're throwing snowballs hoping I'll think it's Kaley as well?"

"My patience is wearing thin," Conrad yelled, scanning the trees with his gun.

Movement caught Sarah's eye. "There," she said and pointed. Conrad followed Sarah's hand. A shadowy figure stepped out from behind a tree and slowly walked through the snow toward Sarah.

"Hands in the air," Conrad said and ran at Philip.

A young man with a mean face threw his hands up into the air. "You didn't have to call my dad," he yelled at Sarah in an upset voice. "I had everything under control!"

Sarah jogged through the snow. When she reached Philip, she stopped. "Where is Kaley Wilson?" she asked, continuing to block her eyes from the snow.

"How would I know?" Philip snapped as Conrad handcuffed his hands behind his back. Dressed only in a tan work coat and a pair of pants, he appeared immune to the icy winds. "She was a waste of my time."

Sarah watched Philip's short blond hair flutter in the wind. "Your father is a good, decent man. How could you betray him?" she asked.

"My dad is a wimp," Philip yelled at Sarah. "Someone in my family has to be a man! Kaley promised that she would take me back to Los Angeles with her. Anything is better than this deadbeat town."

Conrad slapped Philip in the back of the head. "Show some manners, boy," he warned. Philip swung his head around and growled at Conrad.

"Where is Kaley?" Sarah asked, growing impatient.

"Who cares?" Philip snapped at Sarah. "She dumped me, okay? I helped that girl and she broke up with me."

"When did this take place?"

"After I helped her break into your cabin," Philip

admitted in a voice that came out angry instead of guilty. "She found something in one of the rooms...something on your computer..."

"Yesterday?" Sarah asked. "Was it yesterday that you broke into my cabin?"

"No. We broke into your stupid cabin two weeks ago, lady," Philip snarled. "I've been following Kaley... I watched her build that dumb snowman in your yard and break into your cabin again. I watched her throw snowballs at your back door...dumb blond."

Sarah stared at Philip. "Yet here you are, trying to frame Kaley. Why?"

"Because I found her journal in the rental cabin she's living in. She's going to kill you and blame your death on me. And you want to know the kicker?"

"What?"

"I'm supposedly going to kill you because I'm obsessed with the books you write...and I hate reading!" Philip yelled in Sarah's face.

"So you were going to help Kaley kill me before you read her journal, was that it?" Sarah asked.

Philip leaned his face toward Sarah. "No, I was going to kill Kaley and play the hero, lady. I have her tied up in your cabin. Nobody betrays me, especially some stupid blond."

"You are the stupid one," Conrad informed Philip. "And you're in a deep pile of crap."

"So what?" Philip shrugged his shoulders. "My dad will lecture me some, take away my police scanner, and send me to my room. Next week I'll be back at work. The worst that will happen to me is that I'll have to apologize to Fat Girl Rhonda."

"Get him out of here," Sarah told Conrad in a sickened voice. "I'm going to my cabin."

"Not alone you're not," Conrad warned her.

"Alone," Sarah confirmed. "Trust me, okay? I have to go alone."

Conrad stared at Sarah through the snow. Her eyes were watery, her face red and frozen, yet she stood, beautiful and brave, even though it was clear that she was frightened. "Okay, Detective Garland...alone."

"I'll call you when it's over," Sarah promised and walked away toward her Subaru. "Oh, the weather outside is frightful..." She began to hum as the icy winds drowned out her voice.

Sarah eased through the back door of her cabin with her gun drawn and ready to fire. The kitchen light was on. She spotted a pile of rope sitting on the kitchen floor next to a chair and paused. "Kaley?" she called out, closing the back door with her right boot. Silence answered her. "I was very young when I arrested your mother. I was a rookie cop, Kaley. I was only doing my job."

Sarah cautiously moved through the kitchen toward the living room. A warm fire was dancing in the fireplace. "I spoke with Philip. He confessed to everything. I came back to my cabin tonight to help you. He told me he had you tied up here."

Moving through the living room toward the main hallway, Sarah looked down and saw a peppermint candy cane lying on the floor. "Kaley, I'm very sorry about your mother. You need to understand that I was only doing my job."

She looked down the hallway. A line of peppermint candy canes led to her writing room. With her gun at the ready, Sarah walked silently down the hallway and stopped at the writing room door. The door was cracked open. Drawing in a deep breath, she kicked open the door and charged into the room. The window was open, throwing cold wind at the snowman that was standing in the middle of the room. The snowman was wearing a leather jacket and chewing a peppermint candy cane. Sarah nearly screamed.

A piece of computer paper was lying at the foot of the snowman. With shaky hands, Sarah bent down and picked it up. "Gary Hardcastle laughed as he walked away into the woods, eating a peppermint candy cane. Tormenting his victim almost tasted better than the peppermint in his mouth."

Sarah dropped the piece of paper. Unable to restrain her terrified eyes, she looked at the snowman. "You're not real...it's only a story...a story..." she whispered and began backing away from the snowman. "Not real...not real..."

As she backed up into the hallway, Sarah felt a hand touch her shoulder. Screaming, she turned and prepared to fire her gun. Conrad threw his hands up into the air. "It's only me!" he yelled.

"Detective Spencer?" Sarah said, breathing hard.

"It's only me," Conrad promised as he watched tears begin to fall from Sarah's eyes.

"I..." Sarah tried to speak but found that she couldn't. Instead, she buried her face in Conrad's shoulder and began crying.

"Hey, it's all right," Conrad said in a soothing, strong voice. "Everything is all right."

The telephone in the living room rang. Sarah looked up into Conrad's face. "Please, answer the call," she said, wiping at her warm tears.

Conrad let go of Sarah and walked into the living room. "Hello?" he asked, picking up the phone.

"Let me speak to Cat," Peter said in an urgent voice.

"It's your friend from Los Angeles."

Sarah wiped at her tears again, hurried over to Conrad, and took the phone. "Peter?"

"Kaley Wilson is here in Los Angeles," Peter told Sarah. He was sitting in his office, chewing on a cigar. He picked up a cup of coffee, looked at it, and then set the cup back down.

"What?" Sarah asked, confused.

"Kaley Wilson is right here in Los Angeles. She was located at her apartment getting ready for a fashion show that's taking place tonight."

"Are...you sure?" Sarah asked, shocked.

"The young lady is sitting in a questioning room right now," Peter informed her. "I don't know who you've got up there in Alaska with you, but it's not Kaley Wilson. And it wasn't Kaley Wilson who killed her mother, either."

"How do you know?"

"Cat, I wasn't assigned to the Wilson case, so I never

questioned Kaley. But after speaking to her earlier, I can tell you that the young lady really cared for her mother."

"Then who...I mean..." Sarah shook her head as frustration set in. "Then who is building these awful snowmen?"

"I don't know," Peter confessed. "Someone is playing a deadly game with you. You'd better put on your thinking cap and stop acting like a rookie."

"Did you fax the photo of Kaley to me?"

"Yeah, about an hour ago."

"I need you to fax the same photo to the local hospital here in Snow Falls. Call the hospital and get their fax number. Tell them to take the photo to Amanda. She's a close friend of mine. I want the young lady who saw...whoever it is playing this game...to look at the photo."

"Sure thing," Pete promised.

"And then..." Sarah paused as an idea whispered into her troubled mind. "Hey Pete, can you line up a photo set of all the models Kaley Wilson has worked with and send them to me? Talk to Kaley and get all the names of the models she's worked with."

Peter groaned miserably. "I was hoping to get home before midnight, Cat. But, sure, yeah, okay."

"Thanks, Pete. I owe you."

"Yeah, you do. I'll call you when I have the photos ready. And for the love of everything good, keep your blasted cell phone on you."

"I left my purse in my Subaru," Sarah apologized. "Listen, Pete, one more thing," she said in a steady voice.

"Talk with Kaley Wilson and see if she had any enemies, okay?"

"Yeah, you're reading my mind. I'll be in touch."

Sarah put down the phone. "Kaley Wilson is in Los Angeles."

Conrad lifted his right hand and rubbed his jaw. Without saying a word, he walked to Sarah's writing room, examined the snowman and the piece of computer paper lying on the floor, and then returned to the living room. "Okay," he said in a tired voice, "we wait right here. I have Philip handcuffed in a bathroom at the hospital. I called Andrew to go pick him up."

"I told you I needed to come alone. I didn't want to spook Kaley," Sarah told Conrad. Sitting down on her couch, she stared into the warm fire. "In my book, right before Gary Hardcastle finished off his victim, he broke into the victim's home and built a fire in the fireplace."

"Gary Hardcastle dies, though, right?"

Sarah nodded. "The victim, Ruby Whitemoore, kills Gary by chance rather than strength. But, even though it seems to the reader that Gary is dead, I planned on bringing him back in the last book. Now... I'm living out my book..."

Conrad walked to the couch and sat down beside Sarah. "Whoever is behind this will be brought to justice."

"Whoever left that awful snowman in my writing room is out there in the snow," Sarah corrected him. "I guess I need to get a flashlight and go ahead and search for boot prints."

"No," Conrad said and shook his head. "You saw the second snowman on your lawn when you arrived, didn't you?"

"I did," Sarah admitted in a scared voice. "When the third snowman is built...the curtains fall," she explained. "But...Gary Hardcastle attacks when the snow stops falling."

"Exactly," a voice said.

Sarah and Conrad jumped to their feet and swung around. A pretty blond-haired girl was standing in the doorway leading to the kitchen. "Drop your guns," she ordered in a deadly voice.

Sarah locked her eyes on the Glock 17 the girl was aiming at her. "Who are you?" Sarah asked.

"Well, you know that I'm not Kaley Wilson," the girl smiled. Her eyes were vicious. "You can call me Noel."

Conrad soaked in the girl's face, hair, and clothing. She was wearing a pink ski outfit. A long, blond ponytail was flowing out from under the pink ski cap on her head. Pink gloves covered with glitter protected her hands. The girl looked like a model modeling clothes for a ski lodge, not a deadly killer. "Why?" Conrad asked in a calm voice, dropping his gun down onto the couch. He motioned for Sarah to drop her gun as well. "Why are you tracking Detective Garland?"

Noel leaned her head back and laughed. "I don't care about some dried-up prune who writes stupid little books. All I care about is making Kaley Wilson suffer."

"It was you who visited Kaley's Wilson's mother in prison," Sarah said as a sudden revelation struck her mind.

Noel grinned at Sarah. "You're very smart. But not as smart as you think or you would have checked your pantry."

"You tricked Philip into thinking you were Kaley Wilson," Conrad said.

"Yes, I did," Noel said proudly, flashing a pretty smile at Conrad. Conrad didn't find the smile pretty at all. "Philip caught onto my act and decided to play a game of his own. That silly little boy is about as smart as you two are."

"Kaley Wilson is back in Los Angeles sitting in a questioning room," Sarah informed Noel. "Your game is over. There is no way you can frame her for my murder now. And Philip is under arrest. He tried to play your game at the hospital and also attacked an innocent girl."

Noel kept smiling. With her free hand, she reached into the pocket of her ski jacket and pulled out an envelope. "Read," she said and threw the envelope at Conrad.

Conrad bent down slowly and picked up the envelope. Carefully, he extracted a letter and read it. "What does it say?" Sarah asked.

"It's from Kaley Wilson to Noel Dalton, instructing her to kill you...signed with a pen."

"Kaley's actual signature," Noel said proudly. "One night I spiked Kaley's drink. Kaley became, well, a wee bit intoxicated. I had her sign the bottom of that letter for me. Now wasn't that nice of her?"

"So you're going to kill me and send this letter to the police?" Sarah asked.

"That's my plan," Noel answered.

"You killed Kaley Wilson's mother, didn't you?" Sarah asked.

"Yes," Noel said, losing her smile. "Kaley was supposed to take the fall for her mother's death, but the stupid police ruled it as a suicide. But," she continued, forcing a smile back to her deadly eyes, "Ms. Wilson was kind enough to tell me all about how much she despised you, Sarah Garland, and wished you dead. And since mommy dearest didn't help me destroy her daughter, I knew you would have to do."

"Why the games?" Conrad asked.

"Why did you act out my last book?" Sarah added as the winds howled and screamed outside. "You could have easily killed me at any time of your choosing."

"I love your books," Noel told Sarah. Her voice sounded strange. "I love 'The Snowman Killer from Frostworth' series you write. When I found out you were *the* Milly Stevens... oh, it was simply delicious. I couldn't resist the opportunity to play out the part of Gary Hardcastle. I was going to kill you, I really was. But...oh, the weather outside is frightful, but the fire is so delightful...so let it snow, snow, snow!"

"You're a very sick young lady," Sarah said.

Noel stopped smiling. "And you're a dead woman," she promised Sarah. "Into your writing room, Ms. Garland...a.k.a. Milly Stevens."

Conrad nodded at Sarah and walked toward her writing room. Sarah followed. Desperately attempting to think of a way to take down Noel, she glanced over her shoulder. Noel was aiming her gun right at Sarah's back. One wrong move, Sarah knew, and Noel would put a bullet into her.

Sarah walked into the writing room behind Conrad and looked again at the devious snowman. The snowman seemed alive. It stared back at her with dark, shadowy eyes filled with vicious hate. "Now," Noel said, closing the door to the writing room, "before I kill you, I have a favor to ask."

"A favor?" Sarah asked, turning her back to the snowman. Conrad, however, continued to stare at it. He was focused directly on the tree limbs Noel had stuffed into the sides of the snowman as arms.

"Yes," Noel said in a cheerful voice. "I want you to sit down at your desk and write me a short story. I want you to change the ending to your last book. I really didn't like that you killed poor Gary. I want you to bring him back to life."

"I will never bring Gary Hardcastle back to life, not now or ever," Sarah promised.

Noel narrowed her eyes at Sarah and a threatening flash of anger shot over her face. "Bring Gary Hardcastle back to life or I will shoot your detective friend dead," she warned.

"Do it," Conrad told Sarah in a voice that came out calm and even. Noel glanced at him but quickly focused her eyes back on Sarah.

Sarah walked to her writing desk and sat down. The computer was on. A blank writing document was already pulled up. Bowing her head, she closed her eyes. The hideous snowman standing in the middle of the room seemed to be reaching for her mind. The cold winds pouring in through the open window felt as if they were empowering the snowman's desire to torment her. "I...can't..."

"Write," Noel ordered. She walked past the snowman, keeping a safe distance from Conrad, and pressed the gun in her hand against Sarah's left shoulder. "Bring Gary Hardcastle to life!"

Conrad knew it was time to act. He went for the sturdy tree branch sticking out of the right side of the snowman, closest to his body, but before his hand could reach it, Noel swung around and fired a warning shot into the ceiling.

"Listen, handsome," she said in a cold voice, "you're going to die tonight too, so don't rush it, okay?"

Conrad stared at Noel. "You're a very ugly girl," he told her. "Your beauty is as dirty as a sewer rat."

Conrad's insult was like a slap across Noel's face. She aimed her gun at him. "That was very rude of you to say. You're going to pay for that insult, too. Get ready to die, cop!"

"Wait," Sarah yelled, "I'll write...but if you shoot him, I won't. I promise I won't write a single word."

Noel nearly hissed at Sarah. Glaring at Conrad, she lowered her gun. "Write," she ordered again, becoming impatient.

Sarah put her hands together, rubbed her soft, cold chin, and struggled to focus. Hesitantly, she lowered her hands down onto the keyboard and began typing. Conrad watched Sarah write. He watched a truly beautiful and mysterious woman transform into something that his mind could not comprehend—and would never be able to comprehend. The Sarah Garland he knew vanished right before his eyes and Milly Stevens came to life while the snowstorm raged outside, throwing snow into the faces of the two hideous snowmen standing outside like dark, gruesome guards.

"That's it," Noel beamed as she looked over Sarah's shoulder at the computer screen, "bring my love back to life...oh Gary, we're going to be together again."

Sarah closed her eyes as her hands flew across the keyboard. In her mind, she saw the face of a handsome man wearing a black tuxedo. The man grinned at Sarah with perfect teeth and welcomed her with a thick Russian accent.

His eyes were dark and red, his hair black and wavy. "Hello, Sarah..."

"Hello, Gary," Sarah whispered and continued to type. Her fingertips suddenly began changing Gary Hardcastle's appearance. The man's face became ugly, distorted and evil. His teeth became rotted and his hair began to fall out.

"What are you doing?" Noel screamed.

"Showing you the real Gary Hardcastle," Sarah whispered as her fingers flew across the keyboard.

"Stop it...stop it now!" Noel demanded.

"You have to kill me first," Sarah promised.

Noel began to panic. Right before her eyes, she saw Gary Hardcastle transforming into the true monster that he was. Tears began to flow from her eyes. Screaming, she aimed the gun in her hand at Sarah. "Stop it now! Change him back! Change Gary back or die!"

"I don't think so, sweetie," a voice said.

"What?" Noel turned around. A hard fist greeted her pretty face. Stumbling backward, she tumbled down onto Sarah. Dazed from the punch, Noel struggled to understand who had hit her. But before she could move, Conrad had the gun out of her hand and Sarah had thrown her down onto the floor.

"Nice punch," Conrad congratulated Amanda.

"I thought I told you to stay with Rhonda," Sarah told Amanda as she pushed Noel's arms behind her back.

Amanda smiled. "No silly twit was going to get the best of us, Los Angeles. We're partners, remember?"

"I owe you one, partner," Sarah promised. Raising her

eyes upward, she saw the hideous snowman again. "Take her," she told Conrad.

Conrad took hold of Noel. "I've got her."

"Bring him back...bring back Gary," Noel screamed.

Sarah didn't answer Noel. Instead, she walked to the snowman, balled her little hands into two tight fists, and attacked. "I'm not afraid of you... I'm not afraid of you... I'm not afraid of you!" she yelled.

Amanda backed away from Sarah. Conrad pulled Noel to the far corner of the room. He watched Sarah destroy the snowman with angry, brave fists. Snow flew all over the writing room, striking the writing desk, the computer, the walls, the ceiling. "Why did you divorce me...why did you hurt me...why did you hate me?" Sarah began crying as she destroyed the snowman. "Why?" Finally, exhausted from her fight, she dropped to her knees, threw her hands to her face, and wept. "Why?" she whispered.

Amanda walked to her friend, knelt down, and put her arms tenderly around Sarah. Conrad walked Noel out of the writing room. Outside, the snowstorm continued to scream and howl as the world all around Sarah continued to move. In cities far away, couples in love were holding hands and sharing first kisses. But in Snow Falls, Alaska, a brokenhearted woman sat crying in her writing room.

Chapter Fourteen

"Horrible coffee," Conrad whispered to Amanda.

"Drink it," Amanda whispered back, "and eat your cinnamon bun, you ungrateful bloke."

Conrad picked up a delicious cinnamon bun and took a bite. He liked sitting in Sarah's coffee shop. Something about it was soothing to him. "Not bad," he told Amanda.

Amanda brushed cinnamon bun crumbs off the blue dress she was wearing and looked over her shoulder toward the kitchen. "Sarah, love?" she called out.

"I'm coming," Sarah called back. A few seconds later Sarah walked out of the kitchen carrying a fresh pot of coffee. Conrad looked at Sarah and admired how beautiful she looked in the light pink-and-white dress she was wearing. He especially admired how lovely her hair was. Sure, he thought, there were cheap, plastic beauties in the world—but Sarah Garland was the real package.

"What took you so long?" Amanda asked Sarah. "It is a

celebration gathering for solving our case, you know. I didn't get all fancied up for nothing."

"I was on the phone with Peter. Noel...I mean, Hannah Banks...is being transferred to a mental institution in California, compliments of her rich daddy."

"All of this because Hannah Banks was angry at Kaley Wilson over a silly modeling job," Amanda said and rolled her eyes.

"Kaley beat Hannah out of a good job," Sarah explained and picked up a brown coffee mug. She took a sip and winced. "A bit too strong."

"The coffee is perfect," Conrad smiled at Sarah before he could stop himself. Sarah looked at Conrad, gave him a strange look, and smiled back.

"Anyway," Sarah continued, "it seems that Kaley and Hannah had been rivals for quite some time."

"Why didn't Hannah just kill Kaley?" Amanda asked.

"Imagine if you had to sit in prison and watch your rival become the next big model," Sarah explained. "Hannah wanted to torment Kaley."

"I guess," Amanda said and rolled her eyes again. "A bunch of silly twits if you ask me. Speaking of a silly twit, what is going to happen to Philip?"

"Officer Edwin has asked if mercy could be given to his son," Conrad stepped in. "Philip has been ordered to stand up before the entire town, apologize to Rhonda, and explain his actions. If he refuses, it's off to jail with him."

Amanda rolled her eyes a third time. "Silly twit needs to go to jail."

Sarah reached over and patted Amanda on her shoulder. "Down, June Bug."

Conrad listened to the winds howl outside as heavy snow dropped down from a dark, gray sky. He looked at Sarah and began to speak, but just then his cell phone rang. "Hello?... Yes, I see... Okay, thank you." Conrad put away his cell phone. "That was my boss back in New York. He said my old position is open if I want to go back."

Sarah sipped her coffee. She looked at Conrad. Strangely, she didn't want the man to leave Snow Falls. "What will you do?" she asked.

Amanda looked deeply into Conrad's eyes. She knew his answer before he even spoke. "I think I'll stay around a while longer. I still have to find out who killed my ex-wife. Maybe...you can help me...Sarah."

"Maybe...Conrad," Sarah answered back. She looked at Amanda. Amanda smiled at her. "What?" Sarah asked.

"Oh, nothing," Amanda said and took another bite of cinnamon bun.

Miles away, a black limo pulled up to a private jet in Fairbanks. A man wearing a black suit exited the jet, walked to the limo, got in, and told the driver, "Take me to Snow Falls, Alaska. I have unfinished business there."

More from Wendy

Alaska Cozy Mystery Series

Maple Hills Cozy Series

Sweet Shop Cozy Series

Twin Berry Bakery Series

Travel Writer Cozy Mystery Series

Snow Falls, Alaska Cozy Mystery Series

About Wendy Meadows

Wendy Meadows is a USA Today bestselling author whose stories showcase women sleuths. To date, she has published dozens of books, which include her popular Sweetfern Harbor series, Sweet Peach Bakery series, and Alaska Cozy series, to name a few. She lives in the "Granite State" with her husband, two sons, two mini pigs and a lovable Labradoodle.

Join Wendy's newsletter to stay up-to-date with new releases. As a subscriber, you'll also get BLACKVINE MANOR, the complete series, for FREE!

Join Wendy's Newsletter Here
wendymeadows.com/cozy

amazon.com/author/wendymeadows

bookbub.com/profile/wendy-meadows

goodreads.com/wendymeadows

Printed in France by Amazon
Brétigny-sur-Orge, FR

18728206R00070